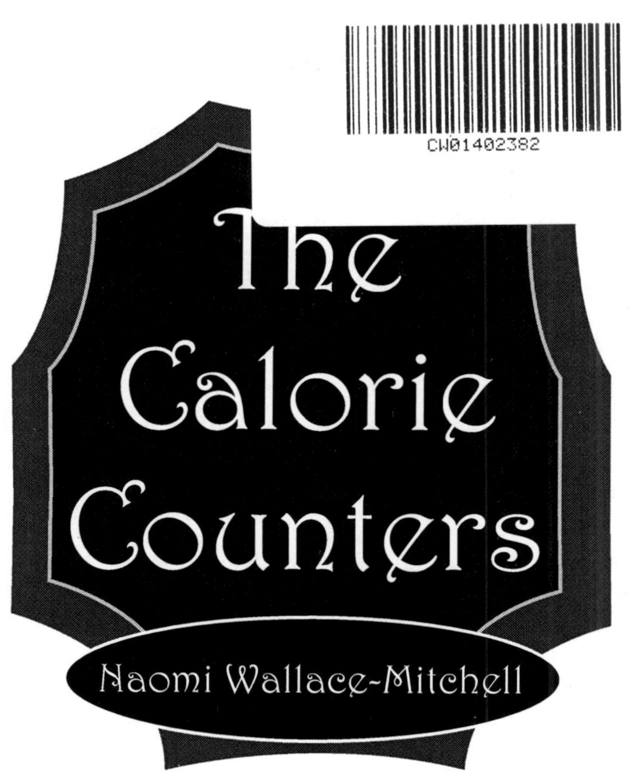

Tate Publishing & *Enterprises*

"The Calorie Counters" by Naomi Wallace-Mitchell

Published in the United States of America
by Tate Publishing, LLC
127 East Trade Center Terrace
Mustang, OK 73064
(888) 361–9473

ISBN: 1-5988629-5-2

060606

To my mother, Margaret
who always supported me in every creative
venture I chose to take. I will always love you.

Introduction

Nothing comes from doing, nothing.
Shakespeare

JUNE MC LEOD AND her husband, Barry had just finished their dinner of fish and chips. As usual, the meal was rather high in fat and salt content and almost non-existent in nutritional value. June excused this by saying,

"It's nice to treat yourself, especially if it makes you feel better."

Barry, who didn't say much at the best of times, nodded his head in agreement. He couldn't care less justifying why they ate it. As long as he had his 'half-a-d' of beers, he was set for the night.

June licked the last of the salt from her fingers, and washed her meal down with a refreshing drink of ice-cold cola. An expression of total satisfaction came over her face as the effervescence of the cola tingled in her throat. Barry let out a loud belch to show his appreciation. He had just devoured five pieces of garfish, one spring roll, and a minimum of chips all to himself.

June wasn't far behind on Barry's intake. She had easily polished off two pieces of whiting, a pineapple fritter, two potato cakes and a minimum of chips. Tonight's meal had cost $35.00. This to anyone else might have seemed excessive. But June excused the expense by stating,

"You've got to eat to live."

The truth of the matter was that Barry and June could probably go for a week without eating anything and be far from dying.

You see Barry and June were what Medical Practitioners call *Obese*.

They were what we would call FAT. Very FAT. They both had a severe weight problem. It would only be a guess (because there wasn't a set of scales in the house) but June weighed around 130 Kilos and Barry was close to 120 kilos.

Barry's mother, Edna had been raised on a farm as a child. She only ever bought pure butter, whole milk and still used lard in her cooking. Anyone who tasted Edna's cooking, whether it was her Sultana scones or her Jam roly-poly, would agree that it was indeed delicious. She was always baking, and one of her servings was enough to feed two grown men. Barry's father had died of a heart attack (not surprising really) when Barry was fifteen. But Edna continued to cook for three. She just divided the servings into halves instead of thirds from then on.

Edna was a jolly woman, eighty-two years of age and the size of a house. She could be found on most days baking in her kitchen, clad in a flour-covered pink frilly apron, stretched beyond its means across her generous breasts. She was always pleased to have a visitor and would lure any unsuspecting doorknocker into the kitchen and promptly seat them at the table for a cupper and whatever she was pulling out of the oven at the time. Be it hot scones with jam and cream or golden egg biscuits.

She was hardly ever short of company, people were

always dropping around. Often Frank the postman or Doug the man who mowed the lawns on Wednesdays. On the days that Edna wasn't home, she would pop around to Barry and June's house with a batch of meringues or whatever she had whipped up that morning. This delivery was never ill received by Barry or June who both loved Edna's cooking. Barry had been a chubby baby that gradually developed into an overweight man as a result of his mother's cooking.

June's family was a little different. She had grown up with her mother, Shirl; father, Ron; grandmother, Agnes; and her two sisters, April and May, all together in the one house. They were a happy family and a caring family. Shirl was very proud of her three daughters and the fact that they were all large girls didn't phase her one bit.

"Big is beautiful," she would say proudly. "My girls are real beauties"

Ron, a shift worker, was as skinny as a rake and not at home much due to his work. He rarely had much to say as Shirl always spoke for the two of them and that suited him fine. They had a happy marriage that worked well for them both.

When Agnes's third husband Mick died, Shirl had welcomed Agnes (Ron's mother) into the house on a permanent basis. Agnes fitted into the family like the proverbial glove.

Agnes, who was now eighty-nine, slightly built like her son and suffering from slight dementia, mostly sat in her old chair looking out the window, chain smoking cigarettes. She would hold a transistor radio to her ear and hum the songs from the "Good old days" to herself. Agnes was no problem at all. And all of Shirl's daughters would take time out in their day to talk to "Nana Ag" (as she was affectionately known) or to read her a story from the newspaper or a condensed novel.

The three sisters were close to one another. April and May lived at home and were both two years apart in age. June was twenty-eight, May twenty-four, and April twenty-two. Shirl had named them after the months that they were born which although went in order of age, conveniently fell on months one after the other.

May worked at the local Savings bank as a teller and showed little interest in the opposite sex. She spent most of her spare time drinking coffee in cafes with her close friends. April on the other hand was the more alternative and academic of the three. She had just completed an arts degree at university with a bachelor in education that had taken four years to complete. She was currently teaching reception level at the local primary school.

April was interested in men, but at this stage she didn't seem to be able to remain in a relationship for more than two weeks. This didn't actually phase April, as she enjoyed going to the pub or to see a band with her friends from University.

It was over-generous servings and the high sugar/ high fat intake that contributed to the girls weight problems, that and little or no exercise. They had dabbled but never persevered in sports at school. Times spent as a family were in front of the television chatting and eating, rather then going outside for a walk or playing a game of beach cricket.

June was the biggest of them all. Over the years the fat had just piled on and on. She had been teased at school for her size, and after a while she just shrugged it off and accepted it as her lot. On many occasions as a child she had been reduced to tears by the school yard taunting bullies, and would console herself by pigging out on a chocolate bar behind the storeroom shed. This developed into a vicious cycle and the problem only increased ten-fold.

• • •

THE ALARM CLOCK chimed on and on in the background for a minute or so until June realized it had gone off. Barry was snoring contently in his bedroom down the hall.

He could probably sleep through an earthquake

She sighed, stretched, searched for her slippers and dragged her large frame with some effort out of bed and trudged down the hallway to Barry's room.

Barry and June slept in separate beds. They were both way too large to sleep comfortably in a bed together. Passion between them hardly existed in their lifestyle. About every one-to-two months June would be awakened by a huffing and puffing, amorous Barry, eager to get into bed with her. She opted for the docile approach, lifting up her nightshirt, allowing him to do his thing. After a short while he would huff, groan, shudder and it was all over. He then gave her a quick squeeze; a kiss on the forehead would let out a big sigh and stumble back to his own bed for the rest of the night. Life continued to go on as normal.

Junes rather non-committal involvement in her husband's sexual advances was not one of disgust or from a bad past experience. She just had little or no self-respect for herself as a human being, which meant that all hope of sexual satisfaction went out-the-window.

Life hadn't always been this way. In the first year that they had married, like most newly weds, they had had sex all the time. Sometimes even twice in the one day! June was much thinner then. (Thinner not thin) and had enjoyed sex very much. Barry was by no means a Casanova or an expert in the fundamentals of lovemaking, but this didn't concern June, as she knew no different. Barry was her first partner, so June had nobody to compare him with. For the first three years of their marriage June had desperately hoped to fall pregnant. She had even sought the advice of a Gynecologist as to why she couldn't conceive. Dr. Carmel's advice was simple.

"You are going to have to reduce your weight before you can even hope to conceive."

The prospect of losing weight appeared such an unreachable task that she became depressed. All her hopes of falling pregnant faded away, as her desire to eat compulsively overtook any other focus in her life. She became more and more dissatisfied with herself and life in general.

CHAPTER 1

If it weren't for the fact that the TV set
and refrigerator are so far apart,
some of us wouldn't get any exercise at all.
Joey Adams

"BARRY, BARRY. Wake up." June begged shaking him by the shoulder.

"Uhh" Barry groaned, "What time is it?"

"Seven-thirty" June replied.

"Oh. Okay thanks luv."

June left Barry's room and headed into the kitchen to prepare their usual breakfast of sausages and eggs.

A little while later Barry emerged from the bathroom, showered and dressed in blue suit trousers, a white shirt and a spotted blue tie, his usual work attire.

Barry worked as a foreman at Mulberry Pty Ltd., a company that specialized in the production of pillow and bed fillings. He had been working there since he was eighteen where he had started in the factory. Over the years he had worked his way up to the position of Dispatch Foreman, which was a rather comfortable but demanding position to hold. It involved supervising the work of three main supervisors who were responsible for twenty-five factory workers each. As long as the factory met its weekly quota, everyone was happy. Because the shareholders were only concerned about high profits and low overheads, Barry had to run a tight ship.

He spent most of his time sorting through inwards goods, shipment documents and consignment forms as well as attending executive meetings. This also included a bi-annual trip to the company's head office, *Soft wear* for a week at a time. Although a little lazy when it came to initiative, Barry was good at his job and his extensive knowledge and expertise accrued over the years of his service was much appreciated by other staff members, who found him to be informative and approachable with staff and company issues.

Barry gobbled down his breakfast, swilled his second cup of coffee, and rose from his chair. Grabbed his briefcase off the floor where it still lay in the place it was dumped last night, gave June a peck on the cheek and announced,

"Well I'm off then Luv."

"What time do you think that you will be home?" June inquired.

"There is a meeting on after work tonight. That will probably go for an hour or so. So I'd say seven seven-thirty? I'll ring you if it looks like going on any later," Barry informed her scratching his head. With that settled, he walked out the door.

June sat down at the breakfast table to her second cup of tea. In the distance she could here the roar of Barry's car as it drove out of the driveway and down the road. She glanced up at the clock on the wall in the kitchen which read eight-thirty five. Then she averted her gaze to a magazine on the table before her. It was one of those real-life magazines with stories about everyday people that also had a variety of puzzles and crosswords to solve.

If you sent the answers away on the form provided you could go into a draw to win lots of different prizes like cars, holidays and electrical appliances. June being an avid reader of the magazine had fallen into the habit of sending her answers away every week as she had done ever since Shirl had first introduced her to the magazine years ago. June was yet to win anything but April had won fifty dollars.

Today, however June wasn't in the mood for solving puzzles or reading about other unfortunates and their miserable lives. The fact of the matter was that she was bored. She was twenty-eight years old, had no children, no job or hobbies of her own, and it was causing her an excessive amount of grief.

It had been three years since her last job as an Accounts Clerk with a small family owned printing firm called *Brady Printing*. June had loved working there and Mr. Brady (who was in his nineties then) was such a lovely man to work for. But his health had got the better of him. Arthritis and de-generation of the muscles had set in along with failing eyesight. It had become impossible for him to continue working and on his doctors advice he decided to sell the business. His children and grandchildren were all involved in their own careers and lives and were not interested in following in his footsteps. The business had been sold and June along with four other employees had lost their jobs.

June found out later that poor Mr. Brady (who had been a very active man in his younger years) had passed away six months after he had finished work. It was commented that he couldn't stand living in a retirement home whilst his mind was still so active. That printing business had meant the *world* to him.

June was keen to find herself another job and had applied for many positions advertised in the local paper. She was called in to attend interviews with four companies. Her resume (which April and May had helped her to compose) was impressive and well presented. But June soon realized that her appearance didn't conform to any of the company's required image. They took one look at her and at how big she was. She knew she didn't any hope of getting the job. It was then that Barry (who was a bit of a chauvinist anyway) decided that it was best if June stayed at home. She tried to compromise with him but the decision had been made and that was it. Barry didn't say much, but when he made a decision on a matter, it was final.

The first few weeks at home weren't too bad. June would visit her parent's house regularly (usually everyday). She had also found ways to entertain herself by browsing at the shops in the local shopping centre or by going to the library. This was until Barry decided that they no longer needed a second car; he had reasoned that by getting rid of June's car they would be saving on the expense of registration, insurance and petrol. Especially now there was only one salary coming in.

It had all made sense at the time. After all June could always catch a bus to her parents' house. There was a bus stop right outside their house. After catching the bus a few times it seemed to work out quite well. That was until that frightful day when time had gotten away from her.

June and Shirl had been perusing over crosswords all afternoon, munching on chocolate biscuits and scorched almonds. June just happened to gaze up at the clock on the video recorder and realized the time was five o'clock. A lot later than the time she usually stayed. June usually tried to get away before three o'clock which was considered off peak time. The buses were almost always empty and the fare was cheaper if you travelled between the times of nine-to-three. Today, however she would be catching the bus during rush hour.

June had gathered up her magazine and handbag, kissed and hugged her mother goodbye and then made her way out the door to the bus stop in the street. Looking at her watch she saw that it was five-thirteen. This meant that a bus would be arriving any moment as they came every fifteen minutes.

It wasn't long before she spied a bus at the top of the hill. She alighted up the stairs, and validated her ticket in the machine. While shuffling up the aisle to find a seat, she'd spotted a group of school children huddled together around the exit door with their bags sprawled all over the floor. She plunked herself down on the last tandem seat available. Huffing and puffing from the sheer exhaustion of moving, June had gathered herself together, opened her magazine and relaxed in anticipation of the journey ahead of her and of finally getting home. It was not long after she had settled in her seat that she had heard one of the school children say,

"Did you see how fat that lady was?"

"Yeah, a real porker," another replied.

"She almost needs a whole bus to herself. Look she's taken up both of those seats, her backside is so wide," one had commented sardonically and they had all sniggered with laughter.

Initially, June hadn't even acknowledged whom they were referring to. Until she turned around behind her to see what all the fuss was about and realized the focus was on her. A sharp pain had gripped at her heart and her stomach felt as if it was doing somersaults inside. The harshness of their taunts and total disrespect for her feelings brought back the memories of her childhood. The callous quips and digs she had endured from the schoolyard bullies. It appeared there was no escaping their cruelty, even in adulthood.

To block out the hurt, and camouflage the tears that welled and threatened to break the levies of her saddened eyes. June desperately tried to use the magazine as a diversion from their conversation. Eventually succeeding, she was surprised by the amount of people that had filled the bus while she had been concentrating on her reading. There were no seats left and hardly any standing room either. She had noticed a young, slender, attractive brunette holding on to the support pole in front of her. The brunette was chatting to a short, petite blond with glasses. June had made eye contact with the brunette, and issued her a friendly smile.

Surprisingly, the brunette had looked her up and down, with a sour expression on her face. Then she turned to her companion and said whilst gesticulating in June's direction,

"Don't you think it is selfish how some people take up both seats?"

"Yeah," her friend agreed. "With all the focus on obesity today and all the low fat stuff you can buy, you would think people would make an effort."

Haughtily, they had both turned towards June and glared at her as if she was a patient in a medical school and they were interns assessing her condition. The blond vainly flicked her hair away from her face, examined her perfectly lacquered fingernails and broke into a conversation about something of an entirely different nature.

June, who had taken almost all one could bear, was dumbfounded. While still recovering from the last upset, this blow to her self-esteem; hit her like a freight train.

Grateful to see the oasis like bus stop approaching,

she had gallantly held herself together, not wanting anyone to see how much it had all affected her. The dense crowds were rather reluctant to move out of her way, but somehow they managed and an emotionally drained June was soon walking up the pavement towards the security that lay behind her front door.

After fumbling for her keys, she finally entered the house and dumped her belongings on the closest chair. She headed straight to the refrigerator and removed a plastic Tupperware container. Upon opening the lid its contents had revealed two cream Kitchener buns. June had greedily pulled them both out, and armed with one in each hand, stuffed them alternately into her mouth.

Then as if all the muscles in her body had given way. Her back had slid down the fridge; her bottom hit the floor and her colossal frame was wracked with uncontrollable sobs.

June shuddered at the recollection; she still felt the pain and humiliation of that awful day so had never caught the bus again. She was reminded every night in her dreams as she tossed and turned in her sleep, trying to escape the pain and humiliation.

She constantly made excuses whenever the subject arose as to why she no longer visited her parents with the regularity of before. One time when Barry had been away on his bi-annual head office visit to Sydney, June had had the use of the car. But that had only been for a week and she had started to become agoraphobic at the thought of getting out and about now that she was used to being indoors. The prospect of going for a walk wasn't even taken into consideration. Not that she had ever been one to walk much. These days if she ever walked as far as the bus stop she was afflicted with a terrible burning sensation between her thighs where her legs chaffed together.

• • •

While gazing out the front window she saw the postman ride past on his scooter. He rapidly fed a bundle of letters into her letterbox and rode on to the next house.

"I had better go and get those," June sighed. She rose with effort out of the chair and made her way to the letterbox, waddling down the path like a duck. Inside again, she detoured towards the kitchen pantry, took out a packet of honey popcorn and sat down at the table. She proceeded to sort through the mail, often stopping to fill her mouth with the sticky, sweet substance. Amongst the mail were a few bills and the usual junk mail. On a red sheet of paper was a pamphlet; written in bold type were the words:

DO YOU NEED TO LOSE WEIGHT?
I CAN HELP YOU NOW.
Call Angela at CALORIE COUNTERS
PH: 055 5555555

June studied the brochure with much deliberation and then with a sudden change of heart, she placed it under the other junk mail out of sight.

The rest of the day she spent watching television, reading and she even managed to have a one-hour nap which was becoming a daily occurrence of late. And that was how her days were spent. Barry was working later then ever and it felt as if they never saw each other. Even on the weekends he would be busy watching football with the guys from work or going over a few things at the office. Their sex life ceased completely and although June noticed, she never took the matter into great consideration.

CHAPTER 2

Be brave. Even if you're not, pretend to be.
No one can tell the difference.

Weight Watchers, Personal Weight Loss Diary

THIS TIME things really began to fall apart, plummeting to an all rock bottom. Barry had just confessed to having an affair with a girl from his work. The girl's name was Mandy, a twenty-five- year old blond, with the body of an exotic dancer, which she used to its full advantage. She spoke in a soft sexy drawn out voice and every word was filled with seduction and sexual innuendo.

June remembered her from Barry's work Christmas functions. She was always the first up on the dance floor and the last to leave. Mandy had a way of grinding and gyrating, her tightly clad body around in a motion on the dance floor that left most men with their tongue hanging out.

Although June had noticed Barry's interest and attentions directed towards Mandy; she hadn't thought much about it because Mandy had that effect on every man in the room. June recalled the time when Mandy had shimmied over to their table, grabbed Barry's (who never danced or did anything very physical) hand and dragged him off to the dance floor, where Barry had made a complete fool of himself. He had no rhythm, two left feet and was drenched in sweat. The perspiration dripped off his beetroot face. He was hypnotized under her spell, and totally oblivious to how pathetic he looked. Afterwards June had to *virtually peel him off the floor*. When the next song started, Mandy had then rushed off to grab the hand of another man whom she hauled onto the dance floor to work her magic on.

June quickly worked out that Mandy chose her dance partners very carefully. She always selected those who held management positions. It didn't take long to figure out that this girl was using her very best assets to further her career. These foolish men were falling into her trap and were caught hook, line and sinker. Barry never spoke of Mandy very often except to mention that Mandy had recently been promoted and that it was the third promotion gained by her in the last three years.

June distinctly recalled the conversation; ironically Barry had remarked how Mandy was a real "go-getter," full of intuition and enthusiasm.

She certainly has that June had thought at the time

There came a time when Barry's hours at work were getting longer and longer, until eventually one night he didn't come home at all. It was after one of those nights that June was woken from a deep sleep at eight in the morning, by hesitant knocking. She had opened the door to reveal a very restless and anxious Barry behind it.

It had occurred to her at the time that it was odd he didn't chose to use his own key, but she had decided not to mention it, sensing that the situation was a bit ambiguous. June remembered that Barry had coyly lifted his head, avoiding eye contact and announced, "Luv we have got to have a talk. Why don't you sit down over there and I'll make us a cupper."

June should have realized that something was seriously amiss as in all their married years; Barry had never offered to make a cupper or lift a finger to help with any domestic chore around the house. Perplexed at this sudden change in her husband's behavior, June had obediently sat down at his request. She then watched as he expertly placed the coffee and a jar of chocolate cream biscuits on the coffee table before her. He had even carefully wiped up the small amount of liquid that had been nervously spilt on the table, rinsed the cloth and neatly placed it back on the sink where it belonged.

June had sipped her coffee, surprised that the only coffee her husband had ever made should taste so good, just the way she liked it white with two sugars. She had found the thought quite touching and a little romantic.

"Who are you? And what have you done with my husband?" June had kidded him.

"Here you might need this Luv," Barry had said as he offered her the jar of biscuits.

"What's this comfort food?" June had asked.

Barry's expression had remained somber and he had sat almost perched on the edge of his chair, looking very uncomfortable. And like the strangers they had become in the last few months they just stared at each other. Thoughts had gone shooting through June's head,

Oh no. He's been demoted, caught drink driving, and lost his license. He's been retrenched. We'll get through it. There's always a way. She reasoned with herself as the thoughts kept filling her head.

Then the bomb had dropped.

"June . . . ahh Luv . . . ahh . . . Mandy and I are having an affair. You know . . . Mandy Hickory. I work with her?"

Huh? June knew who she was all right!

Barry had continued, "We're in love . . . I'm moving in with her. Uhumm," he cleared his throat. "Today." The last word was a faint whisper. He coughed again and clearly announced, "Today - What I mean is. There's no need. You don't have to move out of the house or anything. We'll worry about that business later. When the divorce goes through."

"Mandy*? Divorce*?" June hadn't been sure she was hearing right. "What are *you* talking about?" She was amazed that she had even found her voice. Numbness had come over her and her soul felt strangely removed from its physical self, like an astral spirit, looking down on somebody else's conversation. Then like a bolt of lightening, she realized that the situation was real. Very real!

Barry had risen from his chair, his coffee and biscuit untouched. "I'm just going to chuck a few things together. But I'll be back for the rest," he humbly stated whilst heading towards his bedroom. June had heard his drawers and cupboards opening and closing as he emptied them. And then he re-entered the room.

"I'll be back for the rest in time."

"Where are you staying? I mean, is there any way I can contact you?" she felt desperate. "A telephone number or any thing?" Tears were streaming down June's face.

"I'm staying at Mandy's place. She has a flat. An apartment, she calls it. If you need me for anything, call me at work. I'll get the message. They understand how it is with these things."

"Oh great, always the last to know," June had mumbled sarcastically. Now she was starting to feel angry. "So this is it . . . I mean, our *marriage*?" she had sobbed, trying to make sense of Barry's repugnant news.

"I'm in *love,* June."

More in lust June had thought*, besides, he never called her June, only Luv.*

"Mandy has shown me a whole new life. I mean the

sex. Well that was never really your thing was it? And, now you don't have to worry anymore about me"

He hadn't even said sorry.

"Let's keep it amicable. No hard feelings, hey? I'll keep in touch."

June stared vacantly. He bent down to kiss her cheek. Even though her mind had been on autopilot, she had managed to dodge his kiss. Barry closed the entrance door behind him and was gone. There was no yelling, no bitter exchange of four-letter adjectives, no broken plates. And that had somehow felt worse. In just ten minutes. That was it. Their six-year marriage was over.

CHAPTER 3

For many, life's longest road is the stretch from dependence to independence.
Carla James

JUNE SPENT THE weeks following Barry's earth-shattering confession almost comatose. She couldn't be bothered even getting out of bed, just lazed about all day with the television blaring in the background, crying and feeling sorry for herself. The phone was kept right next to the bed so that she could order take-away. The only time she got up out of bed was to go to the toilet or to get something else to eat.

June had devoured block after block of chocolate, all the chips, biscuits, in fact anything she was able to get her hands (or mouth) onto. She had gained more weight as a result of this. And the food supplies were running out, fast.

June's hygienic standards had dissolved to nothing. She couldn't be bothered having a shower or getting dressed and found standing on her feet caused excruciating pain to shoot up her legs and back. As a result of this she was unable, even to cook a simple meal. Not that she had the energy or the inclination anyway.

The house looked like a bombsite, a complete mess. It was littered with pizza boxes, empty drink bottles, half empty cups of coffee and dirty dishes, scattered from corner to corner.

There hadn't been any form of communication from Barry. It was as if he had completely disappeared. Almost as if their life together had never existed. June found she was having problems, distinguishing between the real and the surreal.

She had received many phone calls from April and May. Shirl called her every day, just to see how she was holding up. June wasn't particularly forthcoming with information. The first time Shirl had called to see how she was going, June had simply said,

"Mum, he's left me. Left me for a girl that he works with."

Her voice had been devoid of emotion. Shirl had decided it would probably be advisable to not question June any further. There would be plenty of time in the future for them to talk. Right now, all June needed was the support of her family network. One thing June had been adamant about was that she didn't want anyone coming around to see her. They had all decided to give her some space, while June remained in her inertial world.

One afternoon, June was in her usual place; bed, watching *Oprah* on the television, when the doorbell rang. "Who can that be?" June muttered to herself, angry that someone had interrupted her private universe.

It took some effort for her to struggle out of bed; by the time she was finally on her feet the visitor was already becoming impatient.

"June. June. Are you there?"

That sounds like Dad. June thought.

"June, are you there mate? It's Dad."

Ron had made a habit of calling all of his daughters, mate. It was an unusual term of endearment, but meant with the best of intentions.

"I'm coming," she grunted as she waddled and gasped for breath to the front door.

And sure enough, there standing at the front entrance, was Ron. He butted his cigarette out, stepping on it with his well worn slip ons to properly extinguish it, wiped his feet on the mat, rubbed his fingers through his hair and entered the house.

"Hi mate! You're Mum was worried about ya. We all are, June." He looked uncomfortable as he made eye contact with her. "I've just finished a shift. I was on my way home, so I thought I would drop in to see how things are, and well. Here I am"

"I'm okay Dad," June replied rather unconvincingly.

"You sure don't look it, not at all. Mum thought you might like to come and stay with us, for a spell?" Ron offered, taking in the image of June before him. Her eyes were red-rimmed and swollen.

"Thanks Dad, but I'd rather stay here."

"When did you last go outside?" Ron enquired looking around the room; he saw dirty dishes and rubbish everywhere. He knew it wasn't like June to be messy and disorganized by nature; her current bohemian and dishevelled appearance worried him greatly. Her condition was definitely much worse then they had thought. He *had* to convince her to come with him and stay at their house.

"Um, I don't know Dad."

June's eyes had started to brim with tears; her father had a way of delving into her inner core and bringing her hidden emotions to the surface. She suspected that this was why her mother had sent him.

"Give us a look at your face. Are you crying Mate?

Come here." Ron opened his arms out and June stepped into his embrace. His arms came nowhere near to meeting around her large girth, but his soothing words of reassurance made June feel loved and safe.

"Come home with us, even if its' just for a couple of weeks? "Your Mum misses you. We all do?"

"Oh Dad I just can't stop crying. I feel . . . I feel so hopeless . . . so." By now she was unable to stem the flow of tears as they cascaded down her chubby cheeks. She looked a sorry sight. Ron, felt close to tears as his heart went out to her.

"I know, mate. I know it's hard. Come on. Come home with me. Pack a few things together. That's the girl. You'll be all right. Mum's got the room ready for you." Ron ran a weathered hand over his chin stubble. "You will come with me then?" he pleaded in one last attempt to persuade her.

June nodded. Ron rummaged through his pocket, pulled out a clean, but very scrunched up handkerchief and offered it to his eldest daughter. She accepted it and blew her nose.

"What are we going to do with you, you poor thing?" Ron said, "Go and throw some things together."

June decided that the idea of staying with her family sounded appealing. She knew she couldn't continue living as she was. She walked into her bedroom and proceeded to fill a suitcase to take with her. As June packed her suitcase she began to realize that most of her clothes didn't fit, and those that did were tight fitting. She decided to pack some t-shirts (size XXL) and her much stretched leggings. Because of her size, she was always hot and rarely felt the cold. Therefore there was rarely any need for jumpers or warm winter clothes.

She spent most of her time wearing a pair of huge

elastic waisted shorts (which she had long ago removed the elastic from as they were too tight) and in a large green t-shirt. They were the only clothes in her possession that fitted her without cutting off her circulation. June had long ago given up on shopping for clothes. The last straw had been when she had gone to enter a clothes shop, the assistant had promptly and not very kindly, told her they had nothing in her size. Scared off by the experience, June had vowed never to go shopping in public again. As a result, she was forced to wear clothes that were ill-fitting, unfashionable and worn-out. June was always pulling her shirts down to try to disguise the rolls of fat on her stomach. Unfortunately, her shirt would immediately spring back onto the moulded outline of her bulk form, emphasizing the shape of her body, again.

"Ready to go are you mate?" Ron enquired when June returned from packing her case.

"I'll take this out to the car while you lock everything up." He picked up her case and headed out the door.

June closed the front door behind her. She felt very exposed as she stepped outside into the open, and walked towards her father's car. The feeling made her anxious and sweaty as well as a little apprehensive about leaving the house that had been her sanctuary over the past weeks. She started to cry again.

"It's okay June," Ron reassured her by patting her left shoulder. June sidled up to the passenger seat and lowered herself down slowly next to Ron. It was a huge effort just moving. The seat was pushed back as far as it would go to accommodate her size. June felt like she had become an invalid and this, added to her already depressed state. Ron started the car and they headed off to her parents house. She left feeling despondent and enervated, nursing her deflated ego like an egg on a spoon.

CHAPTER 4

No one ever injured their eyesight
by looking on the bright side of things.
Weight Watchers, Personal Weight Loss Diary

THE WILLIAM'S HOUSEHOLD was always hectic. It was a complete contrast to the lifestyle that June had been living before. At first she had tried to crawl away and hide in the isolation of her room, however, her family had other ideas. Each time she tried to head in that direction, someone would waylay her in transit and she would be ushered into the TV room or to the dining room table (which was the social epicentre) in an effort to rescue her from dwelling on her problems. It must have had a therapeutic effect on June, as she was slowly starting to feel better. Even if she didn't have much to say, there was always conversation going on around her. Slowly but surely she was starting to relax a little.

It was Sunday morning; June was sitting down at the dining room table, having a cup of tea and munching on a slice of freshly baked Boston bun that Shirl had picked up from the bakery. April walked in; she had just been for a walk around the park. She was on a new health kick and had already lost 10 kilos. June looked up at her youngest sister, enviously admiring her new figure in her close fitting track-suit. April made herself a cup of peppermint tea (all part of the new diet) and sat down at the table opposite June. June pushed the plate, with the Boston bun towards her as an offering. April shook her head, raised her hand in the air declining the offer.

"No thanks. I've got this." She revealed an apple from her coat pocket and immediately began crunching into it.

"So Sis, how are you holding up?" April enquired empathetically. Her face was frowning with concern.

"Oh. Not *too* bad. I guess," June responded unenthusiastically, she was mainly talking to the placemat in front of her, rather then directly to April's face. April had noticed June's eyes fill with tears.

"Listen June, I think you should see someone. A doctor"

June put her hand up to protest.

"No, Just hear me out," April retaliated.

"We are all really worried about you. Mum, Dad, May *and* me. You have been through a lot lately so it's no surprise that you are finding it hard to cope." April slid her chair back and walked around to June's side. She put her arm around her in an effort to comfort her.

"I've got a friend called Dianne Patterson, we went to Uni together. Dianne is a doctor and specializes in women's health in particular. She is very good and understanding." She rubbed June's shoulders affectionately.

"I'll even come with you if you like? What do you say about me making an appointment for you?"

June sniffed loudly into her handkerchief. "Okay" she mumbled dejectedly. "If you think it will help?"

"It's not what I think that counts, June. It's what *you*

want out of life that is important," her tone was filled with authority. "You must admit you are not living a quality life at the moment." April's voice softened, "I'll ring Dianne tonight and have a chat to her."

June nodded. She felt so mentally fatigued that she found it easier to agree than protest. Especially against April who could be very assertive when she put her mind to it.

• • •

TUESDAY MORNING they drove to Dr. Patterson's surgery, for a 10:00am appointment. April had spent an hour and a half on the telephone the night before chatting to the doctor about June's situation and her concern for her.

During the drive, April made many attempts at small talk. She eventually accepted defeat, realizing that she was not getting much of a response out of June. She cranked up the radio and sang along to the music for the rest of the drive, occasionally glancing in June's direction. June's eyes remained focused on the cars and road in front of her. April hoped that Dianne Patterson could be of assistance to June. June desperately needed help, and April was worried that if she was left to her own devices, that June may do something crazy, like attempt suicide. The very thought made her shudder.

When they arrived at the surgery, June gave her personal details to the receptionist who instructed her to take a seat in the waiting room. There were two other patients waiting, a man in his fifties with a moustache who was reading a newspaper and a mousy haired woman glancing at a lifestyle magazine. The woman made eye contact, looking her up and down as she walked past. June, eyes downcast, sauntered past her to get to a seat on the other side of the room. She was feeling very aware of her size. Her heart was pounding and her palms felt clammy. She was beginning to regret ever agreeing to come. April sensing her discomfort handed June a magazine from the teak coloured coffee table in the centre of the room. She selected one for herself and they both sat down and waited. A radio playing music from the classical era was the only sound that could be heard in the background.

Ten minutes passed, and then she heard a faint voice in the distance.

"June Mc Leod."

She looked up to be met with a friendly faced, smiling brunette. The woman was dressed in a tailored business suit; her hair was immaculately coiffed in a French roll.

"Would you like me to come in with you?" April offered, placing her hand affectionately on June's arm.

"No. . . . I'll be fine," June replied shaking her head.

April nodded. June stood up tentatively following Dr. Patterson into her room.

"Take a seat June." The doctor gestured in the direction of a dark green, soft leather sofa. She closed the door behind her and resumed her seat at her incredibly tidy and organized desk.

June took in the conservative but tastefully decorated room with modern art hanging on the walls. Beads of sweat began to appear on her brow as she felt more and more anxious and uncomfortable by the minute.

"My name is Dianne. As you are probably aware, I have been discussing with your sister April, the predicament that you are currently in. April has expressed to me some growing concerns regarding your mental health and general well being" She jotted something on the lined pad in front of her. "Would you agree that there are some concerns?"

June could suddenly no longer contain her self. Tears poured down her face and she began to sob uncontrollably.

The doctor passed June a couple of tissues. She had a genuine look of concern on her face.

"I believe that you are suffering from depression. I am sure that your condition is exacerbated by the unfortunate course of events that you have had to endure." Dianne raised herself from her chair, with her stethoscope in hand. "Can you lift your shirt up please, June? I would like to listen to your heart."

June obliged, feeling total shame as all the fat rolls on her stomach were revealed. Dianne sensed June's discomfort and smiled reassuringly with kind and understanding eyes, as she proceeded to take her blood pressure and announced, "Your blood pressure is much too high for your age and I am concerned about your heart. It is working way too hard. Can you please take your shoes off and stand on the scales over there."

June rose from her chair with great effort and reluctantly stood on the scales before her. Dianne watched her intently, taking in her inability to move freely and her obvious, critical weight problem. June didn't even bother to look at the result on the digital scales. She was past wanting to know.

"Well June, I am going to be very frank with you. You have a serious weight problem. If you do not lose weight you're body will give up as it is under a lot of strain. And you *will* die."

June looked straight into the doctor's eyes and saw that she meant it.

"I am going to give you a referral to a very good nutritionist who operates a weight management program called the *Calorie Counters* her name is Angela Stevens. She is from California, in the US. Where there is a huge problem with obesity. She has had great success with helping patients lose and manage their weight." Dianne adopted a grim expression. "If Angela's method doesn't work for you, we may have to look at the option of surgery and the fitting of a gastric band," she sighed.

"What does that involve?" June asked.

"Well," Dianne pursed her lips, "As well as invasive surgery to fit the band, healing time after the operation, a lot of side effects and a complete change of diet. Some patients even find that they can no longer eat meat."

"What happens if they do? Eat meat, I mean?"

"The gastric band is fitted around the stomach to reduce its capacity. Therefore the gut often becomes ultra-sensitive to certain foods. The gut's reaction is to expel the food from the body. They vomit involuntarily." Dianne paused briefly to allow the seriousness of her words sink in. "This reaction will happen if the patient eats a large quantity of food at a time." Dianne wrote the referral to the nutritionist whilst she explained the procedure to June.

"So, if I don't lose the weight I will have to have one of these bands?" The mere thought of it terrified June, as; she had a very low pain threshold.

Dianne looked up from her writing. "Yes, but only as a last resort. I personally don't like the things. They can cause malnutrition and all sorts of hideous problems if the patient doesn't adhere to a strict eating regime. Any way . . ." she changed tact to a less austere tone. "Let's hope it doesn't come to that." She smiled, handing June the referral and a prescription for anti-depressants.

"*Zoloft*, the anti-depressant, will take a few weeks before you start to feel the benefits. I'd like to see you again in a month. Hopefully we will have you well on the way to a much healthier lifestyle." Dianne opened the door and gently guided June out.

"Thanks. Thank you" June mumbled as she exited the room. There were so many things going on in her head.

Must lose weight -The fitting of a gastric band - The fact that she might die, if she didn't do anything about her weight problem. June fixed up her bill with the receptionist and made an appointment for a month's time. When they were back in the car April asked her how it had gone. June explained everything the doctor had told her. She was interrupted half way through the conversation by another bout of tears. She managed to compose herself and continue.

"Ooh. That gastric band sounds nasty," April admitted.

"Yeah, Well I will do whatever I can to avoid that," June said with conviction.

"Let's drop your prescription off at the chemist and you can make an appointment to see the nutritionist when we get home."

"Thanks April. I don't know what I would have done without you and the others, Mum, Dad and May. Huh, I would probably have gotten so fat that I wouldn't have been able to get out of the house; like those people you see on the *Jerry Springer Show,*" she stated bitterly. "You know the ones that are too huge to come out of a house the conventional way, so they have to remove a wall from a room and then lift them out by crane, because they are totally immobile?"

It sounded so humiliating. April laughed in an attempt to lighten the mood.

"Don't be so hard on yourself, girl"

"I'm not. I am just being honest" June defended

"Do you think you will be able to stick with the diet?" April asked

"I hope so. There is nothing I would love to do better than to lose heaps of weight, be looking good and run into Barry and Mandy."

"Go girl. That's what you need, ammo. That will inspire you to stick with it," April encouraged her. They stopped at the chemist, had June's prescription filled, and then headed home to make the appointment that would change June's life forever.

CHAPTER 5

There are no elevators to success;
you have to take the stairs.
Weight Watchers- Personal Weight Loss Diary

Week#1 - Weight: 130 kgs

JUNE GLANCED UP at the huge sign above the door:

The Calorie Counters (formerly of California)
Angela Stevens- Nutritionist B Sc N& H

Reluctantly she opened the glass door and entered the building. A fresh-faced receptionist greeted her with a welcoming smile as she walked up to the counter. She handed June a folder with a form attached to it and a biro.

"Fill in as much information as you can and then bring it back to me when you are finished. If you find there are any questions that you can't answer or don't understand. I can help you."

June returned the forms to the receptionist and was then instructed to take a seat and wait for Angela Stevens to call her in. In no time at all Angela, a slim woman with salt and pepper hair, and a distinct L.A. accent, invited June to come into her room. June obliged and followed behind her, accepting her offer of a seat in front of her desk. Angela rolled her chair, from behind her desk to June's side and casually sat down, holding the doctor's referral in her hand, adjusted her glasses on the bridge of her nose and quickly scanned the letter.

"Well June. I will explain what we do here exactly."

June shifted nervously on her chair.

"The *Calorie Counters* are a group of people with weight problems who offer support to one another; we also teach healthy eating practices and how to improve your quality of life through weight management and exercise." She cleared her throat. "We design a specific program for each person, tailored to suit their individual needs. We meet every week on Thursdays, where we will weigh you and monitor your progress."

Angela rose from her chair, opened a filing cabinet and handed June a blue folder from there, that was titled the *Calorie Counters*. Pointing to the folder she explained, "In there you will find a more concise explanation about what we offer, along with a support service which is available to you twenty-four hours a day, seven days a week. Now I will get you to hop up on the scales and then we will measure your height to determine what your correct weight should be."

June took her shoes off and stood on the scales.

"130 kilos," Angela said as she wrote the amount down. "Now if you can stand against that wall over there, we will see how tall you are."

June stood in front of the height chart whilst Angela measured her.

"One hundred and sixty-seven centimetres, I'll just consult my chart to see what your ideal weight should be."

She went over to her desk, opened the top draw and took out a black leather bound book.

"It says here your ideal weight should be between sixty-two and sixty-nine kilograms. I think we will aim for sixty-seven kilos, which will mean that you will have to lose sixty-eight kilograms in total."

June gasped "That's more than half of what I am *now.*"

"I know," answered Angela. "It may seem overwhelming now, but we will structure your diet so that you shed one and one half to two kilograms a week. I . . ."

"But that will take *forever,*" June interrupted her.

Angela paused patiently for half a second and continued. "It may appear that way. In the beginning a lot of people find that they will lose three to five kilos per week, but that will stabilize after a while to about one or two kilos per week. Studies have shown that most people, who lose more than that amount in a week, have a higher chance of gaining the weight back in a year or less. I put all my patients on a detoxifying diet to rid your body of toxins and to ensure your liver is working properly. When the liver is cleansed, we can basically re-program your metabolism."

She rubbed the bridge of her nose, underneath her glasses. "I want you to start on the Detox diet immediately for a two- week period. You will have to warn your friends and family to stay away from you for a couple of days, because the detoxifying process can give you headaches and make you irritable."

She noticed June wince and continued, "These symptoms will subside after a few days." Angela stood up. "In that folder you will find the detoxifying diet and tips on suppressing your appetite. There is also a diary, which will teach you how to measure your protein, fat, carbohydrate and fibre intake at your first meeting. Don't worry about starting an intensive exercise program just yet. You might find that you will be feeling quite lethargic in the first week. Have you any questions?"

"Not at the moment," June replied frowning.

"Okay then. We will see you Thursday fortnight, at seven pm." She smiled and opened the office door to let June out of her room. June was just leaving via the front door when she heard,

"Oh and June." It was Angela's voice. "Good luck. Trust yourself. You can do this, I know you can."

"I sure hope so," June said and waved goodbye.

CHAPTER 6

He who has begun his task has half done it.
Horace

JUNE HAD DECIDED to move back home. There had been no word from Barry, so she figured she might as well stay there as long as she possibly could. She had explained to her family that although she appreciated them letting her stay, she felt it was time to be independent again.

June remembered what Angela Stevens had said about the detoxifying diet making her irritable for the first few days, and didn't want to put her family through any-more inconvenience caused by her personal life dramas. She felt enough of a burden to them already.

On the first day of the diet, she set about tidying up the house. She figured that it would be good exercise as well as suppressing the need to eat. Ron had been earlier and mowed the lawns and tidied the yards.

The first two days of the diet, she was only allowed to eat fruit and drink water. The diet allowed her to eat as much fruit as she wanted, and she had spent the day before buying lots of different types of fruit in preparation for the diet. The only fruit she was not allowed to eat were bananas.

June was feeling quite positive and for the first time in ages she felt that she had a purpose in life.

It was six–thirty when she finally put the mop down. She was exhausted, but felt satisfied with the end result. Looking around the house everything shone and sparkled, even the floors. She smelt the body odour emanating from her sweaty body and decided that it would be a good idea to have a refreshing shower.

After the shower, she sat down to a dinner of strawberries, kiwi fruit and rock melon. June found that she actually enjoyed the meal and wondered why she had never taken to fruit before. She helped herself to another helping of the same fruit selection; not long after she was fast asleep in her recliner chair.

The third day of the diet consisted of homemade vegetable soup, any combination of fresh vegetables mixed with some stock and water. June was starting to feel incredibly lethargic; she had a throbbing headache that was only mildly relieved by paracetamol. Her entire body was absolutely screaming for a sugar fix! She persevered though, and by the fifth day she was allowed fruit *and* soup.

By the end of the week June was becoming very creative at making the soup. Some times she used beef, chicken or vegetable stock. Other times, curry or tomato paste, anything to vary the flavour, and make it a bit more interesting. Eventually the headaches subsided and the sugar cravings had gone away, but the feeling of tiredness was still there. Even contemplating anything physical was a big effort.

Watching television, she became aware at how many commercials there was advertising food. This was something she had never noticed before. She felt tempted to splurge on something forbidden such as chocolate, but a determination deep inside her that she never knew existed, would not allow her to.

June's finances were quickly depleting, and without Barry's wage there was nothing incoming. She had decided to sign up for unemployment benefits; one of the provisos for receiving the benefit was that the recipient had to be actively looking for work. She had already decided that she would do this; anyway, in fact she was quite excited at the prospect of being independent again and not having to rely on anyone else. The man at the welfare agency was very helpful and after filling out a lot of forms, promised her that she would begin receiving her benefit in two weeks. June mentally calculated a budget in her head, and realized that her meagre savings balance would probably only last until then. She would just scrape through. June was finding that the new diet cost about one third of the amount that she had previously spent on groceries and if she found a job, without eating take-away food would eventually be able to save some money.

Weight: 127 kgs

JUNE WOKE EARLY on Thursday morning; she prepared her breakfast, which was rock melon, LSA (Ground linseed, soy and almond), plain yogurt, and a glass of vegetable juice. Today was the day of first The *Calorie Counters* meeting. She was feeling ambivalent about going. June had spent most of day had reading through The *Calorie Counters* information leaflets that Angela had given her. After a quick bowl of soup, she made her way into the bedroom to get ready for the first meeting.

She was surprised to find that already her clothes fitted her better and opted to wear a magenta coloured blouse and black pants with an elastic waist that she had not been able to fit into before. This gave her something she hadn't felt in quite a while, a burst of exuberance and an injection of new confidence.

June arrived at the meeting five minutes early. The receptionist, Lillian, gave her a warm welcome, making June immediately feel comfortable. While glancing around the room she saw about twenty people of every shape and size. And the amazing thing was, they were all laughing and having a good time.

"Come on in June," Lillian offered. "I'll introduce you to everyone." Lillian affectionately hooked her arm through June's and led her into the room, where they stopped in front of a very large man with a round beaming face and an equally large woman with incredibly long hair and a wonderful smile. They were engrossed in conversation with Angela. Angela turned around towards June and announced:

"If I can have everybody's attention for a minute please - I would like to introduce our newest member to the group, June Mc Leod."

There was sudden silence and all eyes in the room focused on June. Surprisingly June didn't feel uncomfortable. Everyone looked genuinely pleased to see her and there was a warm and friendly ambiance in the room. A feeling of belonging, that these people would not judge her.

"Hello June," the group chorused.

June gave a coy wave and smiled at their beaming faces.

"Let's sit down and get started shall we?" Angela headed in the direction of a circle of chairs. "There will be time to get acquainted properly, later on."

Everybody found themselves a chair to sit on. June was grateful that the chairs were wide enough to support her. Looking around the room it occurred to her that some of these people would have the same problem finding chairs to fit their size.

Angela sat in the centre of the circle; she looked tiny and ethereal in comparison to the others, but her presence seemed to emanate a type of charismatic power. Every person in the room respectfully gave her their full attention. Angela explained about the *Buddy* system for June and another new member called Michael.

"One of our successful members—i.e. someone who has lost weight and kept it off—is elected as a support coach for each new member. The *Buddy's* main job is to encourage, and offer support to the new member, inside and outside the meeting. The buddy also acts as a go-between; informing me if they think there are any concerns." She glanced at the page in front of her. "Is everyone clear on that?" She looked up at June and Michael for confirmation of their understanding.

They both answered her simultaneously with a nod.

"Kay?"

Kay, a voluptuous woman with flowing titian hair, looked up.

"I have chosen you to be June's Buddy"

"You have been chosen."

A male voice imitated an alien's voice in the background, causing the group to chuckle. Kay gave the man whose name was Tony an austere look, but it was all meant in jest. Every class had a clown. And Tony was theirs.

"And Tony, you are to be Michael's Buddy"

"Watch out Michael, you don't know what you are in for," Kay stirred.

"Well June, you have got the 'Task Master.'" Tony pretended to crack an imaginary whip. The group erupted in laughter again including Angela. When the laughter had subsided Angela asked if anyone had any confessions to make.

"I have. I suppose," a small voice piped up.

Every one turned their attention towards a big blond to the left of Angela.

"Alright Yvonne, what have you got to confess?"

"Well," the woman called Yvonne said, "As you all know I have been doing really well on my diet. I lost nine kilos and all that. But, last Saturday night I went to dinner with the people from my work. And I ate two serves of chocolate mousse for dessert."

"Did you enjoy it?" Angela asked.

"Yes and No. The first couple of mouthfuls were delectable. You know, in fact the first bowl was almost orgasmic. But by the second bowl the guilt started to nag at me, and it kind of didn't taste as good any more." Yvonne screwed up her face, forming a distasteful expression. "And then the next day I was *so* annoyed with myself," she confessed.

Everyone nodded in agreement. It was a familiar scenario to all of them.

"Do you think that you will want to do it again?" Angela inquired.

"No I don't think so. I felt so bad that I was in tears for *most* of the day," Yvonne admitted.

"I guess there is a moral to that story," Angela smiled at all their faces. "No matter how good the idea of eating something taboo is, it never tastes as good as you imagined it to taste."

"Yeah," a few of them replied in unison.

"Oh. I don't know about *that,*" a plump woman Mary spoke above the din of the crowd. "I had a Mars Bar the other day and it tasted wonderful. I didn't have any regrets either," she stated matter-of-factly.

"Yes but you are the only member here that has *put* on weight, instead of losing it," remarked Tony.

They all laughed again, even Mary who knew that she

wasn't very strong in the willpower department. She managed to be philosophical about it though and was therefore often the victim of Tony's teasing which she handled very well. She never appeared to be phased by it at all. Mary was a widow in her late sixties. All of her five children had left home. Recently, Mary had found that she craved adult interaction due to her lonesome life. It was a general consensus among the group that she enjoyed the social aspect of the gathering, more then the prospect of achieving her goal weight.

"Alright I have one more announcement to make and then I will give a short lecture on the different types of fat, such as, saturated, unsaturated, polyunsaturated etc.," Angela announced as an effort to regain everyone's attention. She swivelled her chair around to face Lillian, who was sitting on a table behind the main group. All heads turned towards Lillian's direction. "I am pleased to announce that Lillian has reached her goal weight. For those of you who don't know, Lillian weighed one-hundred kilograms when she first came to us in February last year, and now, after a lot of hard work and dedication, weighs a very attractive sixty kilos." Angela beamed at Lillian with pride.

"Well done Lil. On behalf of *Calorie Counters*, I would like to present you with a one-hundred dollar shopping voucher."

Everyone gasped including Lillian.

"We all know how much you like shopping. Don't we everyone?"

Angela teased her.

"Yes," the group answered as they smiled and clapped proudly. Lillian blushed, and thanked them all. Angela continued with her lecture about different types of fat in food.

When it was over, June realized that she had laughed more in that session then she had in a long, long time . . .

She was even pleased with her weigh in. The scales told her that she had lost three kilos. Kay was by her side.

"You will notice that there are times when you're weight fluctuates a few kilos up or down, but you're clothes will tell you a different story." June listened to Kay intently, as if her words were gospel. Kay continued, "They will tell you that you have lost weight and they will fit better. This is mainly due to the fact that as the fat on you body burns due to weight resistance exercise. You develop muscle tone and muscle weighs more than fat. It is a fallacy that fat turns to muscle. It's physically impossible," Kay told June expertly.

June was glad that Kay was elected to be her Buddy. She felt that they would get on very well. Kay showed June how to fill out her diary and they organized a day and time to commence June's diet regime and set a date for an educational grocery shopping expedition. She found the prospect of this a little daunting but wasn't going to let on to Kay, who sounded so enthusiastic and confident of June's ability to succeed. Much more confident then June felt herself.

June said goodbye to everyone, and headed out the door feeling a different person emerge from within. A huge grin formed across her face, thinking to herself that after seeing all those happy-go-lucky people, smiling must be contagious.

CHAPTER 7

If you smile when no one else is around.
You really mean it.
Andy Rooney, Tribune Media Services

Weight: 125 kgs

JUNE MANAGED TO be strict and adhered to her diet, graduating to more normal type meals, such as grilled fish, steamed vegetables, and tomato-based vegetarian pasta. She was becoming more *au fait* with cooking, finding that she actually looked forward to the preparation of the meal as much as eating it.

Kay took her on an educational tour in the local supermarket. As they walked along, Kay would point out various tips and information about buying low fat, healthy food. She taught June how to read the labels on the back of the products grabbing a packet of savoury biscuits as an example. "The ingredients are listed here on the back of the product." Pointing out with her index finger, "They are listed in the order of the most quantity to the least."

June was looking a little perplexed, so Kay decided to elaborate. "An example would be if sugar is the first or second item listed, you would assume that the product contains a large quantity of sugar in comparison to the other ingredients" June was jotting as much information down on a note pad as she could. "Another trick manufacturers use, is if something is low in sugar, they often substitute the product with more fat or more salt to enhance the flavour."

"But how would I *know* that?" June asked.

"That information is on the back as well. You can tell how many kilojoules, how much fat, how much salt. It's all here on the label. You just have to know how to read it." She went on to explain in more detail as they continued to walk down the aisle, filling up June's trolley with items she had never bought before. Kay stopped at the vegetable oil shelf. She picked up a bottle of olive oil and showed it to June. "See how this bottle says extra light olive oil?" She ran her finger along the label.

June nodded.

"Well that actually means that the oil is light in colour, not kilojoules" Kay confessed to her.

"Really? I would never have known that," June admitted foolishly.

"You're not the only one, everyone falls for that trick" Kay assured her.

When they had filled the trolley full of groceries, they made their way to the checkout. As the checkout operator scanned the items, Kay summed up the tour. "The safest and healthiest way to eat is to buy as much fresh food and vegetables as possible. If a particular vegetable is out of season, the next best thing is frozen vegetables because they are snap frozen, keeping all the nutrition inside." June indicated by nodding that she comprehended. Kay continued, "Like I said, read the labels. Try not to eat anything with a fat content of six grams or more per serve. If you stick to these simple rules, you should be right."

"It's so much to digest," June replied seriously.

"Digest. That's a good one," Kay laughed giving June a playful dig with her elbow.

"Oh yeah, I didn't even intend to say it like that," she admitted while chuckling along with Kay. June paid for her groceries and they pushed the trolley out to Kay's car, giggling like two schoolgirls all the way.

When they arrived at June's house Kay helped her to carry the groceries inside.

"Gee. This is a nice place," Kay commented, looking around the room. "How many bedrooms are there?"

"Three," June answered as she started to put her shopping away.

"Do you live here by yourself?" Kay asked.

"Yeah sort of it belongs to my husband and I. We . . . we're . . ." She cleared her throat. "We are separated." There she had said it.

"Oh. Sorry I didn't mean to pry," Kay apologized as she relaxed comfortably on the lounge chair. "I have a habit of asking personal questions, without realizing that I am offending."

"That's okay," June answered her. "This living alone and separation thing is all a bit new to me. Would you like a tea or a coffee?" June tactfully changed the subject. She didn't want Kay to leave yet as she enjoyed her company and rarely had visitors to the house, but June wasn't ready to talk about Barry quite yet. Kay looked at her watch.

"Yes please, I'll have a quick cupper. Tea, white with none thanks. Do you think you would ever get anyone else in to rent one of the rooms?" Kay inquired as June handed her a cup of tea.

"Why, do you know someone who is interested in renting a room?" June sat down on a single lounge chair next to Kay.

"Yeah I do. Me actually, I live at home, just mum and

myself. We drive each other mad," Kay told her taking a sip of her tea. "Mmm, that's good," she complimented June on the tea.

June tried to conjure up a mental picture of Kay and her mother (whom she had never met) fighting. "Well . . . I suppose I could do with the extra money," she confessed.

"If you were going to, when would you like to move in?"

"Is tomorrow too soon?" Kay suggested earnestly.

"Tomorrow? No that should be alright. . . ." June began to feel exited at the prospect of having a roommate. She supposed Barry wouldn't mind? *Who cares anyway she told herself.* She was feeling a bit decadent. "Come and have a look at the rooms and decide which one you would like. You will have to excuse the mess I'm nearly there, so it should be all gone by tomorrow."

June showed Kay around the house, indicating where the bathroom and laundry was. Kay decided on the bedroom with the light burgundy and cream coloured walls. They agreed on a price for the rent and it was decided that Kay would officially move in the next day.

"Just think . . ." Kay said as she climbed into the front seat of her car. "You will be the only *Calorie Counter* with a live-in, personal trainer." Kay gave June an affectionate jab on the upper arm"Anyway, I'll see you tomorrow, roomy."

June waved goodbye and went back inside to prepare her evening meal. She could feel the winds of change that gently caressed her face.

CHAPTER 8

The key to everything is patience. You get the chicken by hatching the egg, not smashing it.
Arnold Glasow

KAY MOVED HER belongings into the house the next day as promised. June had spent a lot of time preparing the room for her. She wanted to make the right impression and she did. On seeing the room, Kay exclaimed, "Oh! You have done such a wonderful job. You didn't have to go to *so* much trouble."

"Well I couldn't have you moving in to all that mess that was there before. Let's bring the rest of your stuff in, and then we'll have a cupper." Kay gave an eager nod.

After all of Kay's things were neatly arranged in her room, the two women sat down to their cup of tea. They talked excitedly in anticipation of the fun they were going to have living together.

"How about we start your exercise program, this afternoon?" Kay suggested.

"Gee, you're only in the house for an hour and you're already cracking the whip. Maybe Tony is right; you *are* a Task Master?" June teased her.

"Yeah I want you to be dressed in your running gear

and to report to me at fourteen hundred hours precisely!" Kay bellowed in her best sergeant major impersonation.

"Sir, yes sir." June saluted and walked of to her room to get ready, finding it hard to suppress the urge to laugh.

As they stood outside ready to go for a walk, June felt a bit self-conscious in her tracksuit. She couldn't stop pulling the top down to conceal the shape of her body. Kay playfully slapped her hand. "Would you stop doing that? I want your full attention. Now because you haven't done a lot of exercise, the best approach is to take it slowly and build up from there. The most important thing is to do a series of basic stretches, before and after exercise." Kay demonstrated some simple stretch exercises and then indicated for June to join in "This prevents the possibility of an injury occurring due to your muscles not being warmed up."

June tried her hardest to copy Kay but had trouble keeping her balance. She also lacked any form of co-ordination. Kay assisted her as much as she could. When she was satisfied that they had done enough, they began their walk.

"Now we will only go around the block today. Because I sense that you will find this a bit of a struggle at first."

And June did find it a struggle. But she persevered, and with a lot of moaning, groaning and grunting. She eventually made it around the block. When they arrived home, June felt relieved to see her white picket fence. Kay made her do a few cool down exercises before letting her go inside. June was feeling so exhausted and out of breath, that she couldn't even utter a word. She only just managed to crawl through the front door and straight into the bathroom for a shower.

The next day she felt sore and stiff. But Kay was not easily put off. They went for another walk, and then another. Each time, June's fitness improved and she even began to look forward to their morning constitutional.

The new living arrangements also worked out well. They took it in turns to do the cooking and grocery shopping; making sure that they followed their diets to the letter. Whenever June felt down or like she was tempted to quit, Kay was there by her side, gently coaching her and offering her support. Kay was living proof that if June stuck to her guns, her goal really was achievable and that was what kept her going.

CHAPTER 9

It is far more impressive when others discover your good qualities without your help.
Judith Martin

6 months later-Weight 99 kgs

KAY WHO WORKED as a professional hairdresser, eventually convinced June to let her style her hair. As soon as June agreed, Kay set to work, she trimmed, applied a base colour, then foils of colour over the top. When the hair colour was washed out, she finished off with a blow dry of June's new style. The end result was amazing. Even June couldn't believe the transformation that Kay had created on her.

"You look beautiful," Kay complimented her. "You *really* do." She added some finishing touches. June was speechless for a few seconds.

"I can't believe it is me."

"Do you know what?" Kay leant down close to June's ear and whispered, "I reckon that because you have done *such* a good job lately, with your diet and exercising, *and* with you looking so beautiful. We should celebrate with a night on the town, what do you say?"

"Um, I don't know. I . . ." June still couldn't believe that the image she was seeing in the mirror was actually her. She had been on the diet for six months now and had lost over thirty kilos. She slid comfortably into a size eighteen and although she still had along way to go, was past the halfway mark.

"Come on. I'll do your make-up for you," Kay offered in an effort to convince June.

"I don't know what I'm getting myself into, but I'll say yes anyway."

"Good girl. Now let's have a look at your clothes selection, so we can choose something suitable for you to wear."

Kay had literally turned June's wardrobe upside down and emptied all her drawers in a desperate effort to find something suitable for her to wear. "I think the fashion police would lock you up for life if they saw some of these numbers," she stated, holding up a pink angora vest and throwing it on a fast growing pile of rejected clothes. "I think we need to take you shopping. Very soon."

"I know. But what am I going to wear now?" June asked.

"Good question," Kay answered her. "These black pants are all right." She held them up for June to see.

"I don't think they will fit me" June replied.

Kay examined them and then scrutinized June's figure. "You know what June?"

"What?"

"I think you will be pleasantly surprised. Try them on."

June was pleasantly surprised, in fact she was ecstatic. Not only did they fit, there was a little extra room around the waist left for comfort.

"Try this top with it." Kay threw a black embroidered top to June, who keenly snatched it with both hands in mid-flight.

"I don't recognize this one," June said puzzled.

"That's because it's one of mine," Kay replied.

"Oh no, Kay, there is no way this will fit me. I'm heaps bigger then you. You're what, a size twelve or something near to that?"

"This top is a size sixteen. I haven't always been a size twelve you know. Go on try it on. You're smaller in the boobs then me, so it's bound to fit you," Kay encouraged her.

June remembered when Kay told her that she had once weighed one hundred and twenty kilograms. It was hard to imagine Kay ever being obese. She was so lively and motivated. June tried it on, it fitted well and although it felt a little too revealing compared to the clothes that June usually wore, she was impressed with the way it looked. The way she looked.

"Turn around June" Kay instructed, and June obliged.

"I'm not so sure about this," June admitted, pointing to the low neckline on the top, and modestly covering her breasts with her arms.

"Rubbish. It looks lovely," Kay told her, taking her arms away and pulling the top down lower over June's shoulders. "There, that's better."

"Oh. Kay. I don't think . . ." June started to protest.

"Listen June, fat people spend most of their lives trying to cover up their bodies. You have lost a lot of weight, so reward yourself. Its time to start showing it off, girl"

June turned around for one last look in the mirror. "All we need is a pendent to finish it off and a bit of shimmer gloss on your shoulders, now go and have a shower and then I'll do your make-up," Kay said with authority and playfully smacked June on the behind as she walked away.

The taxi stopped outside the nightclub called 'Bennies.' June paid the driver his fare and the girls alighted on to the pavement. For the first time ever, June felt as if she looked half decent. Kay had done a wonderful job with June's hair, and the colours she used on her makeup brought out the lapis lazuli blue in June's eyes. (This was the only feature that she had ever been happy with). Kay looked gorgeous, in a navy blue fitting sheath dress that clung to her every curve. Her golden red hair swished across her back when she moved and her emerald green eyes sparkled with mischief. She was the epitome of a classic seductress.

"Hi Ladies, How are you tonight?" The burly nightclub doorman greeted them. He gave them both the once over, his eyes lingering longer then they should on Kay's exposed cleavage.

"Good, thank you," The girls replied as they paid their entrance fee. The music blared out of the main dance room; June could hear and feel the thud, thud, and thud of the bass as it vibrated through the floorboards. June hadn't frequented nightclubs much before. So this was a whole new experience. There were people everywhere, dancing, drinking, talking and kissing. Some of the dancers appeared to be so absorbed in what they were doing that they were completely oblivious to others around them. It was like a practical lesson in sociology for June, as she watched a group of men up on the balcony above the ladies toilets looking down, hoping to get a glimpse when a woman came out the door. To the right in a dark corner she noticed a couple that were half undressed, becoming very intimate with each other. Across the room she saw what looked like two women having an argument, one of them eventually walking away in tears.

Kay who appeared very much at home in this environment suggested they go to the bar and get a drink. "What would you like to drink?" Kay asked.

June paused as she decided. "A gin and tonic, thanks." She opened her purse and handed Kay a ten - dollar note. Kay shook her head. "No. I'll get this one. You get the next one. It's easier that way." She left June, and headed towards the bar to get their drinks.

June scanned the crowd again. She watched the very vain and the very beautiful trying to capture as much attention as possible. A familiar face came into view, from across the room. June suddenly realized that someone was waving at her. In fact, there were two familiar faces, waving at her. The penny dropped. It was Michael and Tony from the *Calorie Counters*. On seeing June's recognition of them, both men headed across the floor, in her direction.

"Hi. How are you?" June greeted them.

"Well, well, well. Fancy meeting you here," Tony said and he let out a loud wolf whistle. A few other patrons, who were close by, turned around to see what the fuss was about. This caused June to blush.

Michael nodded and smiled at June. He was taking aback by her appearance. He found it hard to keep his eyes off her. He wasn't the sleazy type at all and was always conscious of treating woman with respect. But this had to be an exception to the rule because June was looking absolutely breathtaking tonight.

"Who are you here with?" Tony asked June.

"Kay," June answered him by shouting above the noise. "She's supposed to be getting us a drink, but she must have been held up." She indicated in the direction of the bar. At that moment, June spotted Kay weaving in and out of the crowd, trying not to spill the two drinks in her hand.

"Hi guys," Kay greeted the men. She turned to June

and apologized for taking so long. "I ran into a client from work. She is thinking about getting extensions put on her hair and she was asking my opinion."

"Shall we find somewhere to sit?" Tony suggested.

"How about in the other room?" Kay pointed, "It's quieter in there, so we should be able to hear much better."

"I'll get us a drink, Michael and meet you in there," Tony offered. "Is a beer alright?"

"Great thanks mate." Michael said following in single file behind June and Kay as they headed in the direction of the other room.

Finding a seat at a booth, Kay and June sat on one side and Michael on the other. June discovered that she was sitting directly opposite Michael. She noticed for the first time that Michael had quite handsome features. He was tall with shortly cropped brown hair, and the most striking blue- green eyes and long eyelashes that June had ever seen. Although they saw each other every week at the *Calorie Counters* meetings, they had never really had the chance to talk one on one.

June discovered Michael was very interesting and easy to talk to. They compared notes on their dieting progress and laughed about some of their earlier experiences with exercising and cooking. Michael told her that he had lost thirty kilos and still had another twenty to go. Tony arrived back with their drinks. Michael moved out of the booth to allow Tony in before him. Tony obliged and was soon in a deep conversation with Kay.

"Would you like another one of those?" Michael asked, gesturing to June's empty glass.

"I don't know. The diet and everything," June said reluctantly. The alcohol was making her feel light-headed and more confident than usual and she liked the sensation.

"Oh, don't worry about *that* tonight." Kay said. "You

are allowed to lash out every now and then, as long as you don't do it everyday."

"Yeah, enjoy yourself tonight, June. You and Michael have done really well on your diets," Tony praised them and winked.

"We'll go for two walks tomorrow," Kay promised affectionately squeezing June's hand.

"So I'll take that as a yes?" Michael smiled. "You will have a drink?"

"Yes. I'll have a drink. But this will be my last," June agreed, laughing and rolling her eyes at being so easily persuaded by the majority.

They chatted, sipped their drinks and danced, thoroughly enjoying each other's company. Tony and Kay were getting on very well. June was not surprised by this, as she had sensed the chemistry between them, right from her first *Calorie Counters* meeting. Whilst Michael and June were engrossed in conversation, Kay discreetly interrupted them, asking June if she would accompany her to the toilet to freshen up. June agreed and excusing herself to Michael, followed closely at Kay's heels towards the ladies toilet.

"What's the matter, are you alright?" June asked Kay when they were inside the women's toilets.

"Yeah I'm fine. More than fine actually, Tony has asked me to spend the night with him."

June gasped; she could tell Kay was excited by the way she was talking so fast.

"And what did *you* say?" June pressed her for information. Deep down she was pretty sure she knew the answer.

"I said *yes* of course" Kay replied smugly with her hands on her hips.

"Well you don't need my permission," June stated with a smirk on her face.

"I told Tony that I didn't want to leave you alone. After all we did arrive together."

"I'm not a baby even though I might not be that street-wise" June assured her. "But I *can* find my way home."

"Yeah I know. I just wanted to check with you. That's all."

"Don't worry about me. I'll be fine," June said convincingly.

"You seem to be getting on well with Michael. Is there anything I should know?" Kay teased her.

"We are getting on fine. He's a nice guy. We're not quite at you and Tony's stage yet though," June confessed.

"Oh, so there is potential?"

"You just go and find that man of yours before he thinks you've done a runner on him," June demanded as they made their way back to the two men sitting anxiously at the table. Tony looked relieved when he saw them emerge from the toilet. Kay nodded at Tony then knelt down and grabbed her handbag from under the table.

"We'll see you later," Tony said.

"You sure you are going to be alright?" Kay asked still feeling responsible for June.

"Don't worry. I'll make sure she gets home safely," Michael promised.

"You're a true gentleman Michael," June kidded him, making him smile.

"Alright I'm convinced now," declared Kay. She waved goodbye as Tony linked his arm through hers and they made their way out. Smiling to themselves, Michael and June watched the happy couple walk away.

"Would you be interested in going somewhere for a coffee June?" Michael asked.

"Yes, that would be lovely," she replied, grabbing her coat from behind the chair.

CHAPTER 10

Ultimately, magic finds you if you let it.
Tony Wheeler In Fast Company

MICHAEL PARKED HIS car outside the café that he had suggested they go to, only to find the lights out and the shop closed. "What? This place *never* closes," Michael said with disappointment.

"Look there's a sign on the window." June pointed. "It says, 'Our shop will be closed tonight, due to us attending our daughter Maria's wedding. Sorry if this causes any inconvenience. We will be open tomorrow. Business as usual,' June articulated the message eloquently.

"Of *course*, the wedding is today," Michael remembered.

"Do you know the people who own this shop?" June asked him.

"Yeah I've been coming here for years," he told her. "The Pirelli's are lovely people. I'll introduce you one day. What do we do now? It's still early and I don't feel like going home yet," Michael asked her.

"Why don't we just go back to my house for a coffee? I only live around the corner," June suggested. She was feeling daring. Plus, she trusted Michael and enjoyed his company. Michael agreed as they climbed back into his late model, navy blue commodore sedan. In silence, they drove towards June's house. The night lights had June mesmerised as she battled with a rising fear that she might be doing the wrong thing by inviting a strange man into her house.

"Turn left here" June navigated. Michael followed her instructions and pulled up in the driveway. When he cut the lights, there was a brief moment of darkness and June could only just make out his silhouette against the cars interior. 1–2–3 . . . She conjured up the confidence to take control and invite him into her house.

Inside the lounge room; June handed Michael a mug of hot, steaming coffee and sat down opposite him. He accepted it gratefully and sipped from the cup tentatively. For a brief moment there was silence and June felt a little uncomfortable.

"Have you got any decent music you can put on?" Michael suggested.

"Not really. I only listen to the radio." Barry had taken their entire CD collection with him.

"I've got a great jazz CD in the car; I'll just go and get it if you like?"

"That would be nice."

Michael stood up and went outside to his car to retrieve the CD. June quickly took advantage of Michael's quick departure and went into the bathroom to check on her appearance. She was pleased to see that her make-up and hair still looked all right. When she came back into the lounge room, Michael had the CD playing and the room was filled with the wonderful, relaxing, swinging rhythm of jazz. The distinct melodies made the room feel warm and cosy.

"This sounds great," June admitted truthfully, resuming her seat on the chair. Michael was looking very comfortable, tapping away to the beat with his fingers. His face became serious and he leaned towards her.

"I'd like to say something June. But I don't want to offend you in anyway."

June looked back at him, concerned. A lump started to form in her throat, as she prepared herself for the worse. He continued "I think you look *absolutely* beautiful tonight."

June began to relax again.

"And, I would like to see you again. Take you out to dinner?"

"I'd like that too," June declared giggling nervously. She could feel the adrenalin rising with excitement inside her.

"I'd also like to kiss you, but I don't want you to think me too forward?"

She noticed that Michael's voice was filled with desire. Her mouth opened slightly, as a sign of consent. Sensing her approval, Michael walked towards her, and gently lifted her to her feet. He kissed her softly on the mouth. June responded and they kissed a bit more. She wasn't aware how long they held each other for, but it felt *so* right. His scent was like heaven to her nostrils; natural masculine aroma, blended with a sweet smelling, spicy cologne. It felt *so* nice to be embraced by a man again. Reluctantly, Michael broke away from their union

"I'm going to go now," he said gruffly. "Before we get to the stage where we can't turn back." June agreed. They would be foolish to rush into a sexual relationship so soon. She knew she wasn't ready to cope with anything like that and although she felt drawn to Michael in the way a woman is drawn to a man, she knew it would be a mistake that could not be changed once made. He kissed her on the lips, one more time and picked up his coat. "I'll call you to arrange a time for dinner; does next Wednesday night sound alright?"

"Fine," June told him. She sounded much more confident and composed then she felt. She was on cloud nine, her legs were like jelly and her heart felt as if it was racing a million-miles-an-hour, But, she didn't want Michael to see the affect he was having on her. Little did she know that Michael was going through the same dilemma?

"Bye for now, I had a great time tonight," he whispered as he closed the front door behind him.

"Me too," June whispered back and smiled. She watched him leave from her bedroom window until his car was out of sight. Then, no longer able to contain her excitement, she jumped up and down with joy. That night whilst she slept, her dreams consisted of happy scenes and lots of laughter.

CHAPTER 11

Life is not a laughing matter-
but can you imagine not living without laughing?
Leonid Sukhorukov- In Laughing Matters.

Weight: 98 Kgs

MICHAEL ARRIVED AT six-o-clock on Wednesday to take June out to dinner, as promised. June thought he looked very dapper in his jeans and green moleskin shirt. Michael thought June looked sexy in a red chiffon shirt tied at the waist over black pants with a hint of a bra showing through the shirts transparency. Kay was out with Tony, in fact she spent most her time at Tony's.

"Are you ready to go?" Michael asked her, taking her hand and gently leading her out to the car.

June felt slightly nervous, last Saturday night felt like it was a dream. "Where are you taking me?" June dared to ask him.

Ah, now that's a secret," he answered her mischievously.

"I hope you are not taking me to a restaurant that

serves high calorie food, Michael Carrington?" June was stirring him and he loved her sense of humour.

"We'll actually I thought you liked Mc Donald's?" he responded with a poker face that slowly transformed into a huge grin. She laughed and punched him gently on the left shoulder. She no longer felt nervous any more. Michael looked over at her adoringly and massaged her right shoulder affectionately with his left hand.

They pulled up outside the restaurant. Where Michael went around to June's side and opened the door. She accepted the offer of his hand, as they made their way towards the entrance. June found the restaurant to be beautiful and very classy. She could not remember Barry taking her to one as good as this. In fact Barry hadn't really taken her anywhere much in all the time they were together it suddenly occurred to her as she glanced at Michael reading the menu, that she and Barry didn't really have much in common and that she didn't miss him at all. She was angry about the way they broke up, but now she was feeling relieved that they *had* broken up.

"Have you decided what you would like to eat?" Michael asked her, his aqua eyes looking directly into her own.

"I would like to try the warm Thai chicken salad" she said

"Good choice, I might have on of those as well." He ordered their meals and a bottle of moselle, to accompany the meal. They talked continuously, whilst they ate. Michael told June about his job as an Environment and Development Officer. He also mentioned his ex-wife and spoke about his failed marriage. He told June that although he felt angry when his wife told him she was leaving. That now he realized how unsuitable they were for one another.

"Janine wanted a career. I wanted a family," he said.

"You can't change anyone; I tried to change Janine to my way of thinking. At one stage she even considered having a baby. But she *just* wasn't the maternal type." He sighed shaking his head. "In hindsight I can see that now."

June noticed unshed tears in his eyes and felt both touched and slightly uncomfortable about his open display of sensitivity. She confessed about Barry leaving her for another woman and about how it had made her feel. She also told him how she had arrived at the realization that she didn't love Barry anymore.

They offered each other words of kindness and support and agreed to look towards the future from now on. After a delicious meal and stimulating conversation they agreed to go back to June's house for coffee. Throughout the evening, they had both found it hard to keep their eyes and thoughts off each other as their attraction for one another increased by the minute. June knew that tonight that if they made any form of physical contact, it would definitely lead to them consummating their feelings for one another.

As they walked in the door, they discovered that Kay had not come home. Before she could proceed to the kitchen, Michael embraced her, delaying her from making the coffee.

"I want to kiss you first. I've been wanting to all night," he said as she tilted her head towards him and he took possession of her lips, gently and almost teasing at first. Then as they started to become more intimate, Michael ran his hands over her breasts.

June stiffened under his embrace. Michael sensing the change in her body language unhooked his arms away from around her waist and took a step backwards. He was confused. She had been responding but now she looked petrified. What had he done wrong to offend her? Then she spoke quickly and almost incoherently.

"I'm not ready for this. I don't think I should see you again . . . I think you should go . . ."

"June," he stepped towards her but she put her arms out in defence to prevent him from coming closer.

"I think you should go. I'm sorry Michael. I—" She was trying to be brave. He could see that in her face. Had her husband Barry hurt her that much? The pain and scars were clear in her eyes and by the expression on her face. He had to think quickly. This was one of those situations that could go either way depending on how it was handled. Just one wrong word and that would be it. He liked her. Gosh. He liked her a *lot*. He didn't *want* to leave.

"Please listen to me June," he spoke slowly and gently in order to gain her confidence. He knew he had her attention when she lifted her head up and looked straight in his eyes, her own eyes glistening with tears. She looked vulnerable and all he wanted to do was to hold her and comfort her. It wasn't about sex. He wanted much more than that from her. He sat down on the chair behind him so she didn't feel threatened by his height and attempted to explain to her.

"I'm sorry if I frightened you. I thought you were feeling the same way. I . . ."

"I was," she interrupted him. "At first . . ."

"What I am trying to say is that the physical side of a relationship is not that important at this stage. I will wait until *you* are ready, when *you* feel the time is right.

There are so many things we need to learn about each other yet. Let's not let sex complicate things," he stated hoping he had phrased it right as not to upset her further. She moved a step closer and her body started to relax.

"Truce," he offered and held out his hand to her. She smiled and they connected, shaking hands and instantly repairing any damage that may have been caused earlier to their new relationship.

"Now if you don't mind, I would like to spend some more time with you yet. On your terms though," he suggested gently caressing her fingers with his thumb.

"I'd like that too," she replied and sat down next to him on the lounge chair.

They drank coffee together and watched an old movie on TV. She explained to him as clearly as she could about her reservations for becoming intimate with him but also expressed concern for how that affected him. He reassured her that how it affected him was his problem and he would have to deal with that if he were to become more serious with her; which he wanted to.

As the moon started to shine through the curtains, they realised they had been talking for hours and June suggested he stay over and sleep in the spare third bedroom. He agreed and from then on that become his second home as he often slept more nights at June's house then he did his own. June didn't find it uncomfortable at all. It felt right.

CHAPTER 12

A truly great person is the one
who gives you a chance.
Paul Duffy

Weight: 85 Kgs

KAY HAD MOVED most of her things into Tony's house. She told June that they weren't officially moving in together, but June couldn't tell what was different about it to make it unofficial. She shrugged it off with a smile; she was used to Kay's idiosyncrasies and different perspective on life. It was one of the great things about her personality. June had told Kay to stop paying rent though. There was no sense in her continuing to pay, if she wasn't living there.

Michael spent most nights at June's house except for Fridays. Even though their relationship wasn't physical, June felt more comfortable with him there; but they both agreed they should have one night off to be on their own. June used this night to wax her legs or bleach the hairs on her face. These skills she had learnt from Kay, in the brief time that they had lived together. It was on Friday nights that June missed Kay, even though they saw each other on

Thursdays at the *Calorie Counters* meetings it wasn't the same as when they lived together. She was happy for her though and it was obvious to everybody that Kay and Tony were very much in love. Kay and June took turns alternately in calling each other for a chat on Friday nights. This Friday it was Kay's turn to ring. June answered the phone on the third ring.

"Hello stranger," Kay said in her usual chirpy voice on the other end of the line.

"What's news?"

"Oh not much," June replied almost apathetically.

"I don't believe you," Kay pressured her for information.

"There's nothing to tell," June lied, unconvincingly. There was a pregnant pause.

"Alright we're seeing each other," June confessed, no longer able to contain her excitement.

"And. . . . ?" Kay asked her bluntly.

"Oh *Kay,*" June scolded her, although she was not at all surprised by Kay's bluntness.

"Well. I'm waiting," Kay persevered.

"We seem to be getting along really well." She coughed and cleared her throat. "I like him a lot a *real* lot."

"I *knew* it," Kay responded. "I could tell some thing was going on. You have been positively *glowing* lately."

They discussed a few trivial things, and made an arrangement to go shopping together on Saturday. Michael and Tony had organized to go to a new gymnasium that had recently opened up called *Extreme Health & Fitness.*

"Alright," Kay stated. "I had better go. I have a colour in my hair and it was due to be washed out five minutes ago."

June smiled. Kay was incorrigible.

"I'll see you Saturday, at ten?"

"Yep, bye."

"Bye."

June went to bed early, she was feeling very tired. Since she had joined the *Calorie Counters*, become involved with Michael and made a complete lifestyle change, there wasn't much time for sleep and it was finally catching up with her. But she wouldn't have it any other way she smiled as she drifted off to a contented sleep.

• • •

KAY ARRIVED AT June's house at ten o'clock, as per their arrangement. June walked out with a coat on her arm and her handbag slung over her shoulder. Kay was impressed to see that June had lost more weight on her diet and she told her so.

"Gee girl. You're looking fantastic."

"Thanks," she responded modestly, still not confident in receiving compliments.

"Must be love?" Kay kidded her.

"Yeah, well you'd know." June blushed.

Kay noticed June's face redden and smiled. She had obviously hit the nail on the head. They parked Kay's car in the supermarket car park and entered through the sliding doors, obtained a trolley, glanced at their shopping lists, and chatted to each other about various things whilst grabbing items from the shelves simultaneously.

In front of them there was a man and woman shopping together having a discussion about which gravy they preferred. Kay stared at June. Her face had gone insipid white and she was frozen to the spot.

"What's wrong?" Kay asked her with concern. At the same time the couple turned around to grab a product behind them. June and Kay found they were looking into the faces of Barry and Mandy! There was a short silence, as they continued to stare at each other.

"Hi," June muttered, not sure how to get out of the uncomfortable situation.

"Hi," Barry answered; she could tell he didn't recognize her until an expression of confusion and surprise came over his face. He spoke to her sounding slightly taken aback."June, is that you Luv?"

Mandy was looking impatient as she glanced at June.

"Yes, it's me."

"You're looking fantastic" He selfishly revealed his thoughts aloud, without taking in any consideration of the affect it would have on Mandy. Mandy smiled, but anyone looking more closely would notice that her smile didn't reach her eyes.

"What's you're secret?" she asked. Her inflammatory words were dripping with sarcasm, as she eyed June up and down. June noticed that Mandy had gained a few kilos herself and that Barry was as big as ever.

"Thank you," June replied, knowing she was winning this round.

"Well we had better get going," Mandy said, grabbing Barry by the arm in an effort to drag him away. Barry however, was reluctant to leave, he was totally mesmerized by his ex-wife's new transformation and he ignored her persistent urging to leave.

"I just can't believe it is you," he said again eying June with obvious pleasure.

"It's me," she answered confidently smiling a Cheshire cat smile at him and shrugging her shoulders, nonchalantly.

"I can't stand around talking all day; I've got a manicure appointment at eleven," Mandy demanded abruptly and began to wheel her trolley away. She left, leaving Barry with no option but to follow her. He turned around twice to look at June again as he walked off, still amazed by her new transformation.

June gave him a cool wave and continued on with her shopping. Inside she was trembling.

"I'll take one guess and say that that was your ex and his squeeze?" Kay said crassly.

"You got it in one," June answered her.

"Gee, that Mandy sure is conceited," Kay stated. "I think she was feeling a bit threatened."

"I don't know about that, but I do know that she can keep *him,*" June laughed. Kay joined in, relieved that June was finally getting over Barry, who she personally felt was not worth the tears.

CHAPTER 13

We don't know who we are
until we can see what we can do.
Martha Grimes-in Writer's Handbook

Weight: 81 kgs

MICHAEL AND JUNE lay on the lounge; legs intertwined watching a comedy about a family reunion and all the different problems that occur when very different characters come together all at once. It was very amusing and they both laughed aloud, freely. Michael had cooked June a special meal of curried snapper and rice, followed by fruit salad and yogurt for dessert. The occasion was special because Michael was going to Melbourne the next day on a business trip, and was going to be away for three nights. He had tried every avenue possible to get his employer to let June accompany him. They refused, stating that they were cutting down on expenses and extra partner's expense would no longer be covered. June and Michael accepted this decision as they had no choice otherwise. But they were both feeling disappointed. It was ridiculous; they had only been together for a couple of months. Still the prospect of being apart longer then their agreed *once a weeknight off*, was hard to bear.

"I know you will only be gone for three nights. But I am going to miss you," June confessed to him after the movie had finished.

"I know; me too," Michael agreed. "I will call you every night, and I'll leave my mobile switched on, so that you can call *me* anytime."

They snuggled into each other's arms. In the short time that they had known each other, their feelings had grown so strong. June found she almost had to pinch herself to believe that it was true. She kept expecting to wake up and find that it was all a dream and that she was still one hundred and thirty kilos and living with Barry.

June felt Michaels body language change, and his face wore a serious expression. "Tonight I was hoping I could spend the night in bed with you?" He paused and June's brows knitted together, unsure exactly of what he was asking. "I don't mean make love there's plenty of time for that in the future. I mean that I want to lie next to you all night and just hold you close."

June nodded. She felt that this was something that she would like to. Receiving her consent, Michael gathered her up into his arms and carried her into the room. They kissed and she snuggled into his embrace. They spent most of the night talking, soul searching and revealing their inner thoughts and feelings. June had never felt so close to another human being on an emotional level. It was daunting, but she also felt special and privileged to be given the opportunity to meet someone as extraordinary as Michael, so unlike Barry. And the most amazing thing of all was that Michael seemed to like her. She had been June McLeod who was no one, or so she had thought up till now. Until this *man,* who had made her *someone* again.

As Michael contently snored beside her, she watched his eyelids flutter gently in sleep. With her eyes she trailed his jaw line noticing that it was already beginning to show signs of morning stubble; the perfect formation of a masculine face. Tentatively she reached out and touched his cheek with her finger; she had to convince herself that he was real, that this was not a dream. In response to her touch he smiled and slightly shifted his position. A fly on the wall at that moment would be witness to the pure love that burned in her eyes as she made a revelation with herself, admitting for the first time that her heart had moved on to deeper places.

Michael was in the shower when she awoke the next morning in preparation for his flight to Melbourne later that morning. June gave up her morning walk to spend more time with him.

When it was time to go, they clung to each other in a desperate embrace. They were both averse to separating. When he could delay the trip no longer, Michael finally broke away.

"I'll call you. Tonight," he promised, kissing her one last time. He walked away, deactivated the central locking on his car with a push of a button on his key ring. June watched him from the porch as he opened the boot and placed his luggage in there. Before closing the door of the car to conceal himself behind the slightly tinted windows, he blew June a kiss. She responded by doing the same, watching as he drove off. She remained there for a long time after he had gone staring at the empty driveway, before going back inside the house.

CHAPTER 14

It says something about our times
that we rarely use the word sinful,
except to describe a really good dessert.
Willard Ferrell

JUNE DECIDED TO catch up on her housework. She had neglected it lately, pre-occupied with Michael and her diet. The house had remained reasonably tidy except for the bathroom and toilet, which needed cleaning and the carpet needed a vacuum.

The *Calorie Counters* advocated housework as a form of exercise, so June cleaned the house vigorously. When she was satisfied with the result, she changed into her tracksuit and set off for a long walk down to the local football oval where she would do some laps and stretches.

Arriving home after her walk, she was surprised to see Barry's car in the driveway. Wiping the sweat from her forehead, she did a few cool down exercises and proceeded to make her way into the house. On entering the house she discovered, Barry in the kitchen making a coffee looking, insouciant acting like he hadn't left. June hesitated before confronting him. He turned around and noticed her presence, immediately.

"June. How *are* you?" He greeted her like a long lost friend.

"I'm good and you?" Her answer was cautious and slightly insincere. She was not completely sure of what was going on or where the conversation was heading. In silence Barry continued to make his coffee. When he didn't explain or elaborate any further. June decided that she needed to get cleaned up and changed out of her sweaty work out clothes.

"I've just been for a long walk. I am now going to have a shower and get changed," she announced.

He shrugged his shoulders, unperturbed

When June emerged from her bedroom, dressed in a clean tracksuit she was surprised to see Barry was still there. Looking very comfortable, he was sitting down on one of the recliner chairs, reading her *Calorie Counters* folder. June was beginning to feel annoyed with his apathetic attitude and lack of explanation for turning up so suddenly.

"So . . . What exactly are you here for?" June asked him directly, her hands on her hips.

"It's my house too, you know. I am allowed to be here if I want to," he answered her petulantly.

"I didn't say you couldn't come here or that it wasn't your house," her voice started to rise with anger as she felt herself begin to lose control. She took two deep breaths then, continued in a more controlled voice "I just asked you *why* you were here. Is there any particular reason?"

He looked up at her lustfully. "Gee your looking good these days luv."

"Barry," she said in a slightly whining tone.

"Okay Luv. I thought it was about time we had a talk." He patted the chair next to his. "Come and sit down here June."

To keep the peace and with high hopes that he might

leave soon, June obliged his request and sat down on the chair. "Alright." She let out a big sigh. "What do you want to talk about?" She was very direct with him.

"I just can't get over how much you have changed. Not just looks but, you seem much more confident."

June ignored this comment. Barry was not someone she wanted to spend the afternoon having idle chitchat with. "Get to the point Barry." June couldn't tolerate his presence for much longer.

"What's the aggravation for June? I know things haven't been as good as they could be, between us. But it's not like we ever argued and fought with each other."

He tried to reason with her, but came across as being flippant and insensitive.

June stood up. She was fuming. "Barry, you are such an ignoramus. Do you have *any* idea *how* much you *hurt* me. Do *you*?" She pointed her finger at him with conviction. He dodged her finger by tilting his head to the side.

"What do you mean?" He asked totally unaware of the damage he had done to her.

"Well, you left me for another woman for a start." She took a deep breath. "Not only did you completely destroy our marriage, even though it was in desperate need of assistance. You left me feeling humiliated, unattractive and *so* unwanted. I don't know if I will ever be able to forgive you for that." Tears of anger started to pour down her face and evaporated on her red, hot cheeks before they could make their way any further. "What are you really doing here *anyway*?" she screamed at him.

Barry was stunned by June's sudden outburst and display of wrath. "I was kind of hoping we might try again," he said gently as he leaned over the chair and kissed her passionately on the lips. June felt confused and was totally unprepared for the gesture. When he started to undo his zip on his trousers and lift up her top she tried to push him away, unsuccessfully. Then he was on top of her, pushing her down onto her back.

"You know June? When I look at the new you I feel so hot." His eyes were filled with of a combination of desire and madness.

"Get *off* me Barry" She struggled to get out from underneath him. He continued to grope at her. "Barry it's over. Get off *me,*" she said between gritted teeth.

"You're *still* my wife, June," he snarled as his need to satisfy himself intensified. She attempted again to shift him off, but he was too heavy. Clumsily, he tried to peel off her tracksuit pants and underwear. June could smell alcohol strongly on his breath and she turned her head away in disgust.

"What about Mandy where does she fit into all of this?" she asked in a desperate effort to delay the inevitable.

"What about her? You're still my wife," he replied vulgarly, in a poor effort to justify his actions. June shivered, as a combination of repulsion and fear engulfed her. "Please Barry. *NO*. I don't *wan*t this," she pleaded, urging him to stop. His eyes held a possessive gaze as they bored into her own.

In the background, June thought she could hear a sound like keys jingling, her thoughts were confirmed when the front door burst open and Kay walked in. Kay looked on shocked as she took in the scene before her.

Barry and June stared back at her, mouths agape. Kay realized instantly that June was not consenting to the act. She rushed over to the struggling couple and proceeded to pull Barry off of June with all her might. Barry, who was no longer in control of the situation, sheepishly moved off June and pulled his trousers up quickly. In an effort to cover up, he caught his skin with the zip. Like a wounded puppy, he looked at the two women for sympathy. He was very much mistaken, when Kay bellowed at him.

"It serves you right! I'm going to suggest that June gets a restraining order against you!" Kay's hands were on her hips as she continued defiantly "If I *ever* hear of or see you *anywhere* near June or *this* house. I will personally clobber you myself. You *disgust* me," she spat at him as she stood on tiptoes to reach his eyes.

Barry cowered and winced under her ice-cold stare and vociferous accusations. He looked towards June, who was curled in the foetal position on the lounge, sobbing. "I'm sorry June. I thought you wanted it too?" He said both apologetically *and* pathetically.

"Get *out* Barry" She managed to say with conviction.

He knew by the tone of her voice that she meant it. Humbly, he picked up the rest of his clothes and walked out the door without looking back. He was like a disobedient dog, cowering with his tail between his legs.

After Barry had left the house, Kay perched on the edge of June's chair and gently stroked her hair. June had buried her face into the lounge suite cushion. Her sobbing had subsided and she tilted her head slightly, to meet Kay's eyes. Kay, who could usually talk the pants off a kangaroo, was lost for words. She knew that she had to be sensitive and careful about how she chose her next sentence. She opted for a reassuring approach.

"Well I doubt you will see him for a while." June sniffed in acknowledgement. Kay continued to stoke her hair.

"Is there anything I can get you, a cupper or a brandy, maybe?"

June managed to smirk a little at the last suggestion,

and shook her head. "Some chocolate would be nice," June whispered.

"Did you say *chocolate*? What kind of Buddy would I be if I let . . . ?" Suddenly, she changed tact, realizing that a lecture about high calorie food was inappropriate at this moment "What kind would you like? I suppose you don't have any in the house?"

June shook her head and said, "I would like a family block, of fruit and nut chocolate."

"A family block?" Kay raised her eyebrows. "Alright I'll be back in a sec." She grabbed her car keys off of the coffee table. Before departing on her errand she turned to June, concerned. "Are you going to be alright, by yourself?"

"Yes. I'll lock all the doors behind you. I'm going to have a shower." A look of complete disgust came over her countenance, as she sat up. "I have to wash every *trace* of *him* off of *me*" Her words were filled with hatred and conviction.

Kay placed her hand on June's shoulder. "I'll only be a few minutes, but I'll have my mobile on." Kay's heart went out to June with empathy. "We'll talk when I get back," she said smiling at June. "That is if you feel like it?" Kay hoped that June's silence was an indication of her consent to a discussion, as; she drove out of the driveway making a right hand turn onto the main road.

June turned both taps on the shower to as far as they would go. The hot water was causing condensation to form on the bathroom mirror until there was no reflection in it at all. June stepped into the shower cubicle and gasped as the hot water scalded the tender skin on her back. She scrubbed herself vigorously with the flannel and soap in an effort to rid her self of every trace of Barry's touch. She felt violated and thinking about him made her cringe with disgust. She dry-retched a couple of times as thoughts of him filled her mind. When she thought about them being intimate with each other, she desperately had to fight off the urge to vomit.

As Kay walked in the door she heard the sound of June vomiting. Kay went up to the bathroom door and knocked. "Are you all right in there, June?"

"I'll be out in a minute."

"Okay, I've got your chockie here."

"Yep, I'm getting out now."

"I'll put the kettle on," Kay suggested. It took more than the minute June had promised that she would take. In fact it was more like thirty minutes when she finally came out. Kay had finished her coffee and jumped up to make June a fresh one as hers had gone cold.

"Sit down. This won't take long," Kay instructed. June sat, perched on the end of the chair.

"Thanks," she said as Kay handed her the drink. Kay opened the chocolate block and broke off a generous slab, which she handed to June.

"Now," Kay became serious. "Have you had anything sweet, like chocolate since you have been on your diet?"

June shook her head.

"You will probably find that the taste is a lot stronger then you remember."

June snapped off a square and dipped it into her coffee, a practice she had enjoyed in the past. She waited for the chocolate to melt a little and raising the chocolate to her lips, sucked it into her mouth where it dissolved. Kay watched June intently. When June made no response, Kay asked,

"What do you think? Does it taste different now that you have abstained from it for so long?"

June thought for a few seconds before answering. "It does taste very sweet. A little bit sickening, actually."

"Do you want me to put it away?" June smiled and Kay chuckled as she broke off some more and handed it to June. They dipped, sucked and totally indulged themselves until there wasn't any trace of the chocolate left.

"Just out of interest," June said, "I wonder how many kilojoules there is in a block that size?"

"Yeah," Kay replied, interested. "Where's your *Calorie Counter* book? I'll look it up."

June brought it over to her, looking over her shoulder as she searched. "Here it is." Kay pointed to a page in the book. "Oh you are never going to believe this," she said laughing.

"Go on tell me. I want to know how wicked we have been."

"Alright, there are two-thousand and sixty kilojoules." Her face was full of expression as she read on. "Twenty-six point five grams of fat."

June fell back on the floor laughing. "Twenty *six* point five grams of *fat*?" She said the words again in a syncopated rhythm to emphasize their meaning. "That's almost the total daily recommended fat intake in one *serve!*" June fell back on the floor appearing a little cheerier.

There had been no discussion regarding the incident as of yet, but Kay thought that they were making progress. Now that June was more relaxed, she decided to break the ice.

"How are you feeling? About . . . You know?" Kay saw June clam up after she mentioned it, but was surprised when June confidently said,

"I've thought about it" She coughed and cleared her throat, "I can't *stop* thinking about it. And. Well . . . I'm just going to have to move on." She closed her eyes briefly.

"Are you going to take action against him?"

June shook her head. "No. I just want to see a solicitor and sort it all out."

"That's a good idea. Would you like me to stay over tonight?"

June said she would and Kay rang Tony to tell him she wouldn't be coming home that night. June thanked Kay for being such an understanding and compassionate friend.

CHAPTER 15

The greatest good you can do for another is not just to share your riches but to reveal to him his own.

Benjamin Disraeli

ALTHOUGH THEY HAD spoken on the phone every night whilst he was away, June had not told Michael about the terrible incident with Barry. She had begged Kay (who wasn't keen on the idea), not to say anything to Michael about it.

"I just want to put it all behind me," June had said adamantly to Kay.

That afternoon, June had been to see her solicitor about organizing divorce proceedings. Kay had gone along as moral support. When they were confident that the matter was in good hands, they had decided to go and have a *skinniccino* (similar to a cappuccino, but made with low fat milk) at a local café. Kay brought up the incident again.

"I just think that if you are honest up front. Then things can't turn around and bite you later," she stressed, trying to convince June that she should tell Michael as soon as possible. June would not be persuaded on the situation, so Kay reluctantly decided to leave it up to her.

• • •

MICHAEL WAS DUE to arrive back from his business trip. June had calculated the exact time in minutes that it would take for him to arrive home from the airport. She sat anxiously, waiting for him to knock on the door, regularly glancing at the clock to check the time.

When she heard his car drive into the driveway, she stood up in anticipation of seeing and holding him again. She opened the door forcefully, to reveal him standing there with a suitcase in one hand and his briefcase in the other. He dropped the cases at his sides on the ground and hugged her tightly to him, squeezing her affectionately.

"Mm, you smell good," he said, as he breathed in her clean, fresh scent. June burst into tears, although overwhelmed, she felt safe and secure now that she was back in his arms and the emotion was too much to contain. Michael interpreted her sudden outburst of emotion, as relief to see him, and in some ways that was true.

With Kay's help, June had organised a picnic in the hills. She packed a scrumptious lunch of marinated chicken wings, antipasto, and Greek cheeses slathered on crusty bread. She had also included a small indulgence: a bottle of a locally made crisp white wine that complimented the meal perfectly. She felt decadent and spoilt as the sat on a grassy knoll under a giant gum tree, sipping the wine and tucking into the delicious feast. Michael looked like a king. His face beaming under the dappled rays of the sun shining through the eucalyptus leaves. When they could eat no more, he suggested that they go for a walk along the creeks edge further down. Hand in hand they meandered along the rough path occasionally throwing pieces of bread to a family of ducks that had gathered close. The air was clean, the ambiance tranquil and the company exquisite and they reflected on times not that long ago when they were unable to manage a few steps let alone go for a walk in the country. They made a promise that every weekend they would do something adventurous such as horse or bike riding or even mountain climbing. When it was time to go they reluctantly made their way back to the picnic spot and packed the car ready for home.

For dinner, Michael took June to a quaint little Chinese restaurant positioned on the seafront, which they both enjoyed thoroughly. After their meal they strolled hand in hand along the jetty, comfortable in the warm summer breeze and in each other's company.

Like two teenagers they chased each other across the sand, onto the shore and cuddled in the dark, finding the calling of each others desires harder to ignore.

Michael was due back at work the next day, so they decided to go home and catch up on some sleep. As soon as Michael's head hit the pillow he was snoring gently. Once again, June found herself smiling at his contented features, wondering what he was dreaming of. She lent over and kissed him tenderly on the cheek before turning out her bedside light and going to sleep also.

They were woken the next morning, not by the alarm but by the phone ringing. June glanced at the clock and reached over and grabbed the phone next to her bed.

"Hello," she answered sleepily

"Hello. Can I speak to June Mc Leod please?" a man's voice requested.

"This is she," June replied.

"My name is John Reynolds. I am calling from your local job network. We have a job available that we feel you may be suitable for. The director has looked over your resume and was quite impressed with your skills and references. Are you able to attend an interview today?"

June assured him that she could and John promised to call her back in an hour with a time and address. June thanked him and hung up the phone. When she went back into her bedroom, she discovered Michael was in the shower. She changed out of her pyjamas and set about making breakfast for them both.

• • •

JUNE CAUGHT THE BUS to the interview, aware that she had confronted the demons from the past head on. She no longer had reservations about being out in public. In fact, she thought to her self, smiling, *I no longer care what anyone thinks.*

This notion put a spring in her step as she made her way towards the bus stop. She was looking very chic and businesslike in a black two-piece designer cut suit. The skirt sat just above her knee, it was something that she had bought on a whim with Kay when they had gone shopping. Kay suggested June buy it when she saw her admiring it on the rack. June had relented and although she wasn't sure when or where she would wear it. She was pleased with the fit when she tried it on and even more pleased with the size. Size 14!

The adrenalin rush had been so exciting when she had asked the sales assistant for a size 14. The sales assistant hadn't even battered an eyelid or shown any disgust when she looked at June. In fact she had been most helpful and encouraging towards June in her choice of garment. June had taken the suit home and it had remained hanging in her wardrobe for weeks until now when she had found the occasion to wear it.

Sitting on the bus, June reflected on the many different events that had occurred in her life in the past year since her first appointment with Angela Stevens and the *Calorie Counters.* She would never have dreamed that she would find friends like Kay and Tony and of course Michael. The thought of him caused her cheeks to flush slightly. June had weighed herself that morning and was extremely pleased when the scales revealed a new weight of seventy-seven and a half kilograms.

Lately she felt as if she could conquer the world. Her spirits were completely uplifted. The incident with Barry was only a faint unpleasant memory in her mind, even though it had only occurred weeks ago. June knew that her newfound optimism had helped her get through it as well as the support of her friends. If she managed to get this job she was about to go for, then she would have more then she could ever wish for.

The position called for an experienced receptionist and administrator in an up-market real estate agency, something she would never have even considering applying for before. She knew she had the credentials required and was confident that she could handle the workload. The only drawback this time was that she had been out of the work force for a while, but she already had a reason for that.

She was going to explain to them if they asked her, that she had been unwell and could produce a letter from her doctor if they required it. Stating that she had been temporary debilitated (without going into too much detail) and that she had made a full recovery. She would assure them that it would not affect her ability to work, or her work performance in any way. Going over everything in her mind, June felt quite confident. She only hoped that she would be able to convince the interviewer, when it came to the crunch.

June saw her destination approaching, she pressed the buzzer to indicate to the driver that she wanted to get off at the next stop. Out on the pavement she made her way in the direction of the real estate agency. She remembered a time long ago when she and Barry had delighted in glancing in the window and looking at all the grand and expensive homes for sale and rent; one of the few times in the relationship that she felt some degree of happiness.

The front of the shop was decorated in a federation theme and was painted navy blue and cream. As she entered through the door she saw that the same theme was continued inside along, giving a classy and stylish effect. June walked up to the main desk and notified the receptionist of her appointment. The receptionist was very professional but amicable in her manner, and June noticed when she stood up to get something off the laser printer that she was also heavily pregnant with child. After she resumed her seat, she asked June to fill out a few details, while she telephoned the interviewer to tell her that June had arrived.

June sat nervously, her legs shaking slightly under her skirt. She crossed her legs to help settle them, aware that she was showing a generous amount of thigh. The phone on the reception desk rang and soon after the receptionist informed June that the interviewer was ready to see her and gave her directions to an office down the passage way. June knocked on the door.

"Come in," a refined voice reverberated back at her. She opened the door to see a woman with a blond bob, dressed in tweed tailored jacket and camel coloured moleskin jeans. The woman was selecting a book from a Baltic pine stained bookshelf. June watched as she perused the book briefly before setting it down on the high-gloss, maple desk in front of her. The woman turned around as June entered the room.

"Well hello there," she greeted June in a friendly manner. "June, I take it?"

"Yes," June smiled back at her.

"Take a seat June. Make yourself comfortable." The woman leaned over the desk and shook June's hand, firmly. "I am Charlotte Sinclair, director of the company. Pleased to meet you."

June could tell by her mannerisms, that Charlotte was a woman who was confident and used to dealing in what was predominantly a men's world. She could also tell that Charlotte was a no-nonsense person and would expect total dedication and efficiency from her staff. This however did not dissuade June. In fact it made her want the job more. Charlotte was the kind of woman people tried hard to impress.

"I've had a good read of your resume, June. You have most if not all of the qualifications that we are looking for." She tapped the black fountain pen in her hand on her desk, rhythmically. "Your references are excellent. I took the liberty of calling all your referees this morning and I am pleased to say that they all give you glowing reports."

"That's good" June replied, completely taken in by this woman's presence and style. Everything about Charlotte screamed professionalism, and sophistication.

Charlotte asked her some general questions about her work experience and quizzed her on what her positive and negative attributes were. Satisfied that she had enough information, Charlotte announced, "I'll be honest with you, June. The decision is between you and another person. I will discuss this further with my colleagues and let you know by . . . Lets see . . ." She consulted the calendar on her desk, "Friday. I am sorry to make you wait that long but I am going to Sydney tonight and won't be back until Wednesday."

June nodded her acceptance. They shook hands again and June left the room not really sure if the interview had been successful or not. She glanced at her wristwatch. The time was two-fifteen. Michael had asked her to call in and have lunch with him if she was out in time. She decided to call him when she got home to apologize for not making it she knew he would understand. That's what she liked about him the most. He was *so,* understanding.

And oh *so* perfect!!

CHAPTER 16

A leader takes people where they want to go.
A great leader takes people where they don't
necessarily want to go, but ought to be.
Rosalynn Carter

Weight: 73 ½ kgs

MICHAEL AND JUNE walked hand in hand towards the *Calorie Counter* premises. When they entered the building, June was surprised to see two new members present. The group took their regular positions on chairs in a circle around Angela.

"Hi everyone how are we all feeling today?" She scanned the room in a clockwise motion.

"Gooood," the group chorused back.

"Glad to hear it -We have two new members tonight. On my left is Kyla and on my right is Cara."

The group chorused their usual hello and the two women each waved, shyly back. Angela gave her usual speech on the Buddy system, explaining everything it entailed and how it worked. For some reason June found her mind was drifting away from what Angela was saying. It was probably because she had heard the Buddy system being explained every week for months on end. She was startled back to attention when she heard Angela announce,

"June, I would like you to be Cara's buddy."

June looked in the direction of the woman called Cara. She was a large woman with shortly cropped hair that did nothing for her, except to emphasize how fat she was. June gave her a welcoming smile. Cara smiled nervously back. It occurred to June that this woman was probably a carbon copy of herself fourteen months ago when she had first joined the *Calorie Counters*.

"I have two more announcements to make and then we will begin tonight's lecture on complex carbohydrates," Angela said as she turned around to Lillian who was sitting on the table behind her. Lillian walked over to Angela and handed her two envelopes. Angela thanked her and continued with her announcement. "I am very pleased to announce that we have two members who have reached goal weight tonight, Tony and Kay."

Everyone clapped and Tony imitated an exaggerated bow. Angela handed them their envelopes, which each contained gift vouchers. Tony's had a hardware voucher and Kay's contained a shopping voucher. After the lecture, June helped Cara weigh herself and they organized a time to go shopping at the supermarket together. Tony and Kay invited all the members to their house for a barbeque they were having next month. Everyone said they would try there hardest to come along.

• • •

JUNE HAD ARRANGED with Cara to pick her up from her house on Saturday morning. Michael had lent her his car and she felt very privileged to be given the opportunity. Michael had let her drive the car once before after they had been out for dinner. He had been drinking red wine with his dinner and was concerned that he might have been over the legal alcohol limit. June had only had one glass of white wine at the time. As she drove to Clara's house today, she felt very independent. This was the first time she had driven a car by herself since Barry had left.

June also felt in control of her life. Especially after seeing Kay and Tony reach goal weight. This had made her realize how far she had come with her diet and with her life. And now she was going to be someone's Buddy, a mentor, offering guidance to someone else. She felt very important.

She left her thoughts to concentrate on finding Cara's house. Slowing the car down she spotted a red brick house with a curving driveway to be number twenty-nine. As she pulled into the driveway she saw Cara come out of the house. June smiled at her.

"Hi. How are you?"

"Good. Thanks," Cara replied and proceeded to open the passenger door. June realized immediately that Cara was not going to fit in the seat. June got out and adjusted the seat to as far back as it would go. June could tell that Cara felt embarrassed by this and she silently cursed herself for not thinking of it before she left home.

As they were driving along in the car, June enquired as to how Cara was going with her detoxifying diet. Cara wasn't very forthcoming with information so June asked "Are you finding that you are hungry in between meals?"

Cara was in tears. "I just can't seem to be able to stick with it. I got these *awful* headaches. They drove me mad and then I couldn't stop craving sugar and. . . . It's just been *so* terrible. I can't *do* it." She sounded *so* desperate.

"What exactly are you finding to be a problem, maybe I can help you?" June offered.

"I just can't stick with it. No matter how hard I try,"

she sobbed. "The first two days I craved sugar *so* much that I went out and bought a packet of chocolate biscuits . . . I just don't think I can do it."

June parked the car outside the supermarket. She switched off the ignition and turned to Cara. "I know it's hard. Believe me. But you have to persevere with it. Come on, let's go inside," June suggested indicating towards the supermarket. They walked around the supermarket, June explaining to Cara as much information as she could offer about eating and selecting the right food. June had the feeling that Cara wasn't really interested or paying attention. She also found that Cara was very negative about dieting and losing weight. June felt she was fighting a losing battle. She made a mental note to call Kay when she got home and to ask her advice about how to approach the situation. Kay had been such an inspiration to her that she hoped that she could help.

June dropped Cara off at home and helped her inside with her shopping. Cara offered June a coffee. She was about to decline when she changed her mind, hoping that by staying she might be able to offer Cara more encouragement and change her attitude to a more optimistic one.

She sat at the kitchen table and watched Cara prepare the coffees. She noticed that Cara heaped three spoons of sugar into her own coffee and June shook her head in disbelief. This was going to be tough. Her thoughts were confirmed when Cara offered her a sweet biscuit from a cookie jar. June declined but Cara helped herself to three.

"Cara. Do you realize that you can't eat biscuits and have sugar in your coffee if you hope to lose weight?"

"Yeah I know. It's just that I've always had sugar in my coffee and I love dunking biscuits while I'm drinking it."

June was feeling a bit annoyed and thought it was

time she left, before she said anything that she might regret. "Listen to me Cara. I can't help you if you *won't* help yourself."

Cara looked down at her feet and nodded like a naughty school child that had just been chastised for doing something wrong.

"Call me if you need anything. Or even if you just want to talk."

Cara nodded again and June left, saying goodbye as she walked out the door.

When she got home she called Kay immediately, hoping that her best friend could offer some suggestions about what to do. Kay listened intently to June on the other end of the phone as she explained the situation and her concerns about Cara.

"Sounds like you have a tough one there," Kay replied. "I think that all you can do is support her, be there for her and encourage her. If that doesn't work, you may have to talk with Angela about it."

"I was thinking that," June agreed, mainly in response to talking to Angela about the situation.

"I mean, I know it sounds harsh, but you can't *make* her lose weight if she won't do it herself or if she doesn't want to. Your job is to educate her on how to do it and to support her. But it's up to *her* to do it"

"So do you think I should give her another week and see how she goes? If she is still having problems or won't try, then I'll talk to Angela?" June was feeling better now that she was talking to Kay. Even though Kay could not offer her a direct solution it was obvious. The ball was in Cara's court.

"That's all you can do. Let me know how you go and call me if you need to talk," Kay offered.

"Alright, thanks Kay," June said as she hung up the

phone, still pondering to herself about how she was going to handle part two of the situation with Cara. *But I do like a challenge she thought to herself.* This was certainly going to be a challenge, but she had overcome higher obstacles before.

CHAPTER 17

I have failed over and over again in my life.
And that is why I succeed.
Michael Jordan

JUNE WAS AWOKEN from a deep sleep, by the phone ringing. Sleepily she answered it. “Hello?”

“Hello June, it’s Charlotte Sinclair speaking. I was wondering if you would be able to attend a second interview today.”

June thought for a minute, trying not to sound sleepy and incoherent. “Yes. That would be fine, Charlotte. What time?” She put on the best professional voice she could muster.

“How about let me see . . . is two o’clock suitable?”

“Yes. Two would be fine.”

“Great. We’ll see you then. Bye June”

“Bye.” As she hung up the phone she considered going back to bed, but now the idea of possibly getting the job she really wanted was just too exciting to go to sleep. This was a rare morning when Michael hadn’t stayed over. He had spent the night at his own home as his mother was over for the weekend from Bendigo, Michael’s hometown.

June was going to Michael's for dinner that night, so that she could be formally introduced to his mother, Caitlin.

June was very aware that Michael was yet to meet her immediate family. Her excuse to herself was that she didn't want to appear too pushy with Michael by introducing him to her family so soon. They had been together for over seven months now. June was worried that Michael might feel as if she was trying to force him into marrying her and she didn't want to scare him off, because it was a thought she hadn't even considered. In fact the prospect of marriage to June at this stage was quite daunting and full of bad experiences. She was quite enjoying the single life.

June ate her breakfast, washed and rinsed the few dishes she had in the sink and was about to go for her morning walk when there was a knock at the door. She opened the door to reveal Edna Mc Leod. Edna was dressed up in a full, blue print dress. She was carrying a Tupperware container in her arms. When she saw the metamorphosis in June she was amazed and surprised.

"Oh Junie, I can't believe it is really you. You look wonderful!"

"Thanks Edna," June said kissing her on the cheek. Edna took the liberty of embracing June. June hugged her back. She loved this kind and gentle natured woman. "Come inside. Would you like a cup of tea? The kettle has just boiled."

"Yes dear. I would like that very much." Edna followed June into the kitchen. "I'm so sorry I haven't called earlier. I meant to," Edna looked away, bashfully.

"It's okay," June tried to reassure her. "It's not your fault." June placed the two cups of tea on a silver tray along with the meringues that Edna had brought along. She carried the tray into the lounge room and placed it on the coffee table.

When they were sitting down and sipping their tea. Edna offered June one of her meringues. June declined but Edna insisted that she needed fattening up. June thought to herself how ironic that was when she had spent so much time and effort trying to lose weight. She politely took one meringue, even though she didn't really feel like one. She nibbled on it slowly as Edna spoke.

"June, this really is such a shame between yourself, and Barry. I'm sure you can work something out. I . . ."

"Edna. I know he is your son and I love you dearly. But Barry left me for another woman and well . . . we have both moved on in our lives," June explained democratically.

"I know Barry left you for another woman dear, it won't last. His father, Bill was a womanizer but he always came back to me. Couldn't resist my cooking, he said."

"I'm sorry Edna." June attempted to explain without offending Edna too much. "There is absolutely no chance that Barry and I will ever get back together again. You're always welcome here anytime. Even after the divorce I would still like to stay in touch."

Tears were brimming in Edna's eyes as she looked up at June. "*Divorce.* I guess you have made up your mind then?"

June nodded; she wasn't going to upset Edna by telling her how Barry had tried to rape her. "I am happy, really happy Edna, with my life and everything."

"Alright then dear, I'd best be going now. Doug is coming to mow the lawns today and I have to bake some sultana scones for him. He likes them."

June smiled. She sensed that Edna's feelings for Doug ran deeper than she openly let on. "Thank you so much for visiting me." June kissed her on the cheek. "Remember, you are always welcome."

"You too dear, you're always welcome." Tears welled

up in her eyes again as she made her departure. June gave her one last hug before closing the door.

Later on, June prepared for her job interview. She was feeling slightly melancholy after Edna's visit. It wasn't that she wanted to be back with Barry anymore. She was *adamant* about that. It was just sad when things ended. Especially, in a relationship between married couples, where you not only lost the partner that you had hoped to spend the rest of your life with, but you also lost the partner's relatives and friends.

June was certain that she would not see Edna again. It would be no fault of either party. In the first few years, they might send Christmas cards, or talk on the phone occasionally. June knew how it worked. Then there would come a time when their contact would gradually dwindle away. This was what was making her sad. It was as if she was morning the loss of a loved one. In fact, in a way she was.

CHAPTER 18

Friends are the family you choose
Jennifer Aniston in Esquire

JUNE SAT ACROSS the maple wood desk once again, staring at Charlotte Sinclair. Charlotte was tapping figures into a calculator in front of her. She jotted a few numbers down on a pad, picked up her phone and tucked it under her chin so that her hands were free to write. She glanced over at June.

"Please excuse me June. This won't take a minute." Her focus went back to the telephone. June assumed that someone had spoken at the other end of the phone as Charlotte's next words were. "Miriam. It's Charlotte Sinclair speaking. I have gone over the figures again. We can accept an offer of seven hundred and fifty thousand for the Jolly- Whites property." June watched Charlotte with awe. She was so confident and professional. "Alright, run that by them and let me know what they say. Okay, thanks Miriam. Bye." She hung up the phone. Her full attention was now on June.

"Well June, I have one question to ask you."

"Yes?" June answered her attentively.

"Can you start on Monday?"

There was a brief pause as June finally registered what exactly Charlotte was offering. "Are you saying that I have got the *job*?" June asked trying not to sound too excited.

"That is exactly what I am saying," Charlotte smiled at her. "We will put you on a three month probationary period. That is the norm these days."

"What does that entail, exactly?" June asked.

"After a period of three months, if we are not happy with you or *you* are not happy with *us*, we, go our own separate ways." She said it so matter-of-factly that to some degree, it terrified June. "Let's hope it won't come to that," Charlotte said as she rose from behind her desk. "We'll see you on Monday at eight o'clock sharp." Charlotte opened her office door to let June out. As she walked past her, June caught a whiff of Charlotte's expensive French perfume. "Bye June. Welcome aboard."

"Bye," June said turning around in Charlotte's direction. Charlotte had already resumed her position at her desk and was talking business to someone on the phone. June knew that Charlotte would expect June's dedication and pound of flesh as an employee. But she also realised how insignificant she was in comparison to the big wide world of business, which Charlotte delved in on a daily basis. June could live with that. It was going to be a great opportunity. She was so pleased to get the job that she ran all the way to the bus stop.

When June got home she saw that there were two messages waiting for her on the answering machine. The first message was from Michael. He had called to wish her luck at her interview and to finalize the arrangements for dinner with his mother that night. The second message was of a more distressing nature. It was from June's mother, Shirl. Nana Ag had suffered a huge stoke and had passed away at nine that morning.

The bad news took all the wind out of June's sail in regards to her job offer. She was suffering feelings of guilt about neglecting her family ever since her relationship with Michael had started. In fact her family hadn't *even* met him. She picked up the phone to call her mother back and offer the family her condolences. She was also going to have to ring Michael and cancel their dinner with his mother. It was a shame that she was not going to meet Caitlin. She would have to catch up with her next time she was in town. Right now there was a funeral to organize and that involved the whole William's family.

• • •

MICHAEL EXPERTLY PARKED the car in the last parking spot available in the funeral parlour car park. He and June walked across the white stoned pathway, passing beautiful landscaped gardens as they made their way to the main building. A friendly man met them at the entrance and ushered them into an area, which had church pews set out in rows and a podium at the front. June spotted her family assembled in the front row of the room. The service was just starting so they opted for a seat towards the back as not to cause any unnecessary distraction.

"We are gathered here today to remember and celebrate the life of Agatha Maeve Williams."

They all listened attentively as the reverend delivered a lovely service dedicated to Nana Ag. He talked about her life achievements and her involvement in the Second World War as a casualty nurse and the perils of this responsibility. He spoke of her character and of her friends and family, taking all who was present on an interesting and emotional journey of her life.

When the service was over, each member was asked

to place a red carnation (her favourite flower) inside the casket as they exited the room. As they passed the coffin, a trumpet player belted out the notes to "The Last Post" in tribute to Nana Ag's service in the war. June thought that Nana Ag looked peaceful in the casket and she said so to Michael as they paid their respects and placed their flowers beside her.

All friends and family gathered in a main area of the establishment where they could mingle as they were served tea and coffee and light refreshments. June saw people there that she remembered from when she was a little girl. The people's bodies had aged since she remembered, but she recognized their eyes. That was how she could tell who they were. The eyes never aged.

Everyone talked about Nana Ag as she was, passionate, strong willed and very determined by nature. They laughed as they remembered her little quirks and idiosyncrasies. Many remarked at what a good, long life she had lived. June shed a few tears like many because they would miss her, but she knew as they all did that Nana Ag had enjoyed a good life. In fact the last few years she had suffered from dementia, so her quality of life had been reduced quite significantly. Most agreed that her passing was a blessing in disguise.

June quickly grabbed her parent's attention at the first opportunity she could get to introduce them to Michael. They were constantly inundated with people wanting to talk to them and catch up with them after many years of not seeing each other. When she saw a woman walk away from Shirl and Ron, June seized the moment by moving in before anyone else could.

"Mum, Dad. This is Michael. A friend of mine."

"Pleased to meet you Michael," Shirl said smiling at him. She could tell that Michael was more then a friend to

June because both of their eyes were glowing when they looked at each other. Shirl felt like a weight had been lifted off of her shoulders. June had come such a long way in the past six months and now she was sure that she was going to be okay. Ron shook hands with Michael.

"Sorry you had to meet us under these circumstances, mate," he said.

"That's okay," Michael assured him. "I'm just sorry I didn't meet your mother when she was alive."

Ron smiled and nodded in acknowledgement of the depth of Michael's words. He had decided that he liked him already.

"We would like you all to come back to our house today for a wake and a little bit of lunch. Do you think you will?" Shirl asked them.

"Of course we will, Mum" June said speaking for the both of them. Michael gave his confirmation by smiling warmly with his eyes.

"Can I get a ride with you?" April asked as she moved in on the conversation.

"Hi, I'm April by the way. You must be Michael?"

He nodded. "Hi April, you are quite welcome to get a ride with us if you like."

"And me too," May came over to join the conversation.

"This is my sister May," June introduced them.

"The more the merrier," Michael invited.

As they made their way to the car; Michael and June held hands, which didn't go unnoticed by the Williams women, who followed closely behind them, smiling to each other a kind of conspiracy of acceptance.

• • •

THE WAKE WAS celebrated in true William's fashion. Nana Ag would not have wanted it any other way. Shirl was in her element walking around with food platters, coaxing people to eat far more than they wanted or should. There was plenty of food to eat and lots of alcohol to drink. June and Michael were probably the most sober of all the people present. Michael had to drive and June didn't want to consume too many calories. She was getting very close to goal weight now and didn't want to throw any obstacles in the way of achieving it. She sipped slowly on a glass of white wine that lasted her for most of the afternoon.

April, on the other hand, had consumed quite a few wines. June could tell because she always became very chatty and deep and meaningful in conversation when she was inebriated. April noticed June looking over in her direction. She stumbled over to June and sat by her side.

"Hi Junie, How are you going?" She was slurring a little.

"Good, thank you April," June answered her.

"Michael seems like a nice guy and cute too. You have done very well," April praised her.

"Yes. He's the best thing that has every happened to me." As June spoke she watched Michael talking to Ron across the other side of the room. Michael felt her gaze on him and turned to her and smiled. June smiled back.

"I spoke to Dianne the other day and she was saying how pleased she is with your progress."

"I know. I feel on top of the world at the moment. I keep thinking I am going to wake up to discover that it was all a dream," June admitted.

April nodded her head "I know what you mean. But you deserve it. You have done it all by your own merits."

"What about you April, is there any romance in your life at the moment?"

"Yes, a teacher from school. The only problem is that he is married," April whispered in June's ear.

"Oh April, you'll end up getting hurt."

"I know, but I like him so much. And he is going through a bad stage with his wife. Apparently they live completely separate lives. Only together for the children . . ." Her face held a dreamy, faraway expression as she spoke.

"Just be careful," June warned her and hugged her gently. Michael walked over and joined in the conversation.

As they were leaving Shirl and Ron extended the invitation to Michael to visit them whenever he wanted.

"That means that they like you," June told him affectionately as they drove home in the car.

CHAPTER 19

Honesty is probably the sexiest thing
a man can give a woman
Debra Messing in Esquire

JUNE AND MICHAEL were the last to arrive at Tony and Kay's house for the barbeque. They had been held up because Michael's car had a flat tyre. Michael had gotten so much grease all over his hands and shirt that they had to go home again so that he could clean up and get changed. The party was already in full swing in the backyard. When Kay sighted them arriving, she rushed straight up to June.

"I thought you guys would never arrive," she said sounding agitated and anxious. June couldn't understand what all the fuss was about. It was only a casual barbeque.

The answer came to them later on in the afternoon when Tony and Kay mysteriously disappeared inside the house emerging about twenty minutes later. What happened next was breathtaking. Kay was dressed in a white sleeveless bridal gown that showed her curves off to perfection. She carried a nosegay of iceberg roses and her hair had been neatly piled on top of her head A few loose tendrils of hair curled past her ears in ringlets to soften the effect. June thought she had never seen her looking more beautiful.

Tony must have thought so too, dressed in a dark green tuxedo his gaze was filled with adoration as his eyes remained firmly fixed on Kay, oblivious to anyone else. Every one gasped when they realized what was about to take place. June thought to herself that there was nothing more magic then seeing two people who were so in love with one another. It was like an honour to be able to witness it.

A female celebrant dressed in Indian styled flowing robes, appeared from behind the crowd and the exchanging of vows commenced. When the ceremony was over, Michael and June were asked to come forward and witness the union by signing the marriage certificate. They obliged wholeheartedly. When they were done the celebrant turned to the gathering of people and announced "I would like to introduce Mr. and Mrs. Lavers."

The crowd clapped and the party continued as everyone stepped up to the newlyweds and offered their congratulations. June went up to them both. She hugged Kay and kissed Tony on the cheek.

"You devils," she teased them. "What did you think you were doing by throwing a surprise like that on us?"

"We didn't want everybody to make a fuss. So we thought that this was the best way," Kay explained.

"We could have eloped to Bali or somewhere like that, but it isn't the same without your friends," Tony said.

"You're not getting all sentimental on us are you, mate?" Michael teased.

"So what if I am?" Tony replied and they all laughed together. June mingled with the other guests. There were a lot of people from the *Calorie Counters* there. Some of the newer members told her what an inspiration she was to them and she felt elated by their compliments. June noticed Cara on the other side of the yard, sitting down on her own, tucking into a large slice of Pavlova and cream. She shook her head and raised her eyebrows at Angela who had also noticed.

June and Angela had a long chat about Cara and her lack of discipline in regards to her weight management. June had tried other tactics suggested by Angela but to no avail. Angela told June that she had a long discussion with Cara about her goals and lack of enthusiasm, health concerns etc and had decided to relinquish June's responsibility to Cara as a Buddy. She claimed that Cara was not about to help herself, so June shouldn't get upset about not being able to help her either. Her advice was fairly similar to Kay's. But June felt quite relieved at not having to carry the responsibility of Cara, as it was the only thing in her life that was getting her down.

Just as she was thinking about her, Cara came over to June to say hello. When asked about her dieting progress, Cara became defensive, excusing herself for eating the Pavlova. She told June that she was going to have a gastric band fitted and was living it up before she had the operation.

June wasn't surprised to hear that Cara was having the band fitted. She knew that Cara's doctor would have to do something drastic in order to get Cara to lose weight as her health was at risk the way that she was.

June felt disappointed in Cara. Her lack of will power had caused her to take drastic measures to reduce weight. June was sure that Cara would find the whole experience unpleasant.

Angela had explained to June when she had raised her concerns about Cara's lack of drive, how some people aren't able to stick to any controlled eating regime. No matter how dire the consequences! Angela had described these people as "food addicts" explaining that they were similar to cigarette smokers, alcoholics and gamblers. They were all driven by the same insatiable desire to pursue their addiction, whatever the cost. June remembered how hard it had been to change her eating patterns and lifestyle but still she had persevered in the end. She shuddered at the thought of how awful it would have been if she had not succeeded.

"You're miles away," Cara said to her annoyed. "You weren't listening to a *word* I said."

"What? Oh, sorry," June apologized. She had no idea what Cara had been talking about for the past few minutes.

"I was saying that you have lost a lot of weight," Cara told her enviously. June detected a vicious undertone in the way Cara spoke about June's weight loss. It was then that it occurred to June that she didn't really care for Cara's company very much. June looked around the yard for a possible escape from Cara and was relieved when she saw Tony and Michael in deep conversation next to the barbeque. June willed Michael to notice her. When he eventually did she waved at him and he waved to her. June used this routine to tactfully excuse herself from Cara, claiming that Michael was trying to attract her attention. As she headed towards the two men she was curious to find out what they were discussing that was so secretive.

"What's the reason for this *tête-à-tête*? June asked them.

"I didn't know you could speak French," Tony said.

"Now that she is working for *Sinclair and Associates* June has become multilingual *and* Continental," Michael kidded her.

June made a face at him. "You guys are changing the subject. I want to know what you were talking about that was so secretive."

"It's not what, but who," Michael answered her.

"Who? What are you on about?" June was intrigued. Michael lent closer to her so that he could whisper in her ear.

"Now when I tell you I want you to promise that you don't look over in their direction."

"Whose dir . . . ?"

"Shoosh," Michael hushed her, putting a finger to his lips.

"We were discussing the relationship between Angela and Lillian."

"What relationship?" June was puzzled.

"They are an item. You know lovers."

"Lovers, Lesbians?" June raised her voice with surprise.

"Quiet," Tony said to her.

"I didn't know Angela was gay," June confessed.

"Who's gay?" Kay asked interrupting the conversation as she collected plates from the trestle tables.

"Angela and Lillian" June whispered in her ear. "They're an item."

"I know," Kay responded. "Lillian told me."

"Well there you go," June stated.

"There you go," the other three chorused with her and they all laughed. Kay and Tony went off to get changed. They had called a taxi to take them to the airport. They were going to Fiji for their honeymoon and would be away for a week. Everyone crowded around the taxi to see them off.

"We are going to show off our newly sculpted bods," Kay joked as she climbed into the taxi and everyone laughed.

"Just don't make that bikini too skimpy or you'll be up for a divorce," someone heckled back at her.

"I won't," Tony replied and every one joined in the laughter as they waved goodbye to the newlyweds.

Tony and Kay had suggested that every one stay on at their place and continue the party after they had gone. Michael and June had agreed to lock the house up and along with a few other friends, they were coming back the next day to tidy up the mess and restore the house and yard to its former state.

CHAPTER 20

Successful people are very lucky.
Just ask any failure.
Michael Levine, Lessons at the halfway point

Weight 67 Kgs - Goal Weight!

EVERY ONE GATHERED around June at the *Calorie Counters* meeting, Angela made the announcement. "I have great pleasure in presenting this award. This person has come a long way in a not so very long time," Angela's Californian drawl emphasized the words so much more. "When she came to me in May this year I must confess I wasn't sure that she could go through with the whole weight management plan. But she proved me wrong. She was also disagreeable when I told her she should only lose one kilo a week. And again she proved me wrong." Angela was beaming with pride as she talked. "I must admit that I am glad to have been proven wrong." She paused as everyone laughed. "June Mc Leod, on behalf of everyone at *Calorie Counters* we are honoured to present you with the award of reaching your goal weight in a safe but record time. You have lost sixty-eight kilos in seventeen months. Come on everyone; give her a round of applause," Angela encouraged the group.

June gazed at all the smiling, proud faces that looked on at her with pride. Lillian handed her a shopping voucher along with a huge A1 size certificate for reaching goal weight in record time. Suddenly it seemed as if people were appearing from everywhere. There was Kay, Tony, her parents, sisters and of course, Michael. *Good, strong reliable, solid as a rock Michael.* Each one came up and congratulated her for achieving her goal. They toasted her success with sparkling sugar-free apple juice and mineral water while they nibbled on pieces of healthy food such as carrot, capsicum, celery, raw mushrooms and reduced-fat cheese served with a low fat hummus dip and a platter of fresh fruit.

June had never felt so happy and complete. All the people she loved were gathered around to celebrate her reaching the hardest goal she had achieved in her life. Things had changed, so dramatically that she couldn't really remember the heartache, the frustration and the dissatisfaction that she had suffered from before she had embarked on this amazing and yes, challenging journey. But what she could remember, be it a minute glimpse of her past, was enough to keep her going on the new path she had found without ever needing to worry about turning back.

"A speech," Tony heckled. "A speech."

"Okay, okay." June stood up, feeling on top of the world. Everyone clapped. "Firstly, I would like to say thank you to all of you, especially those who encouraged me and helped me get through the hard times. And to those of you new members who are feeling overwhelmed by the size of your task, I will quote for you something that helped me get through each day. I photocopied it lots of times and pasted it in just about every room of my house. I read it in a magazine once and it stuck with me. It's from a woman called Abigail Van Burenand and was published in the Universal Press Syndicate. I know this because I have read it many times a day."

Everyone laughed at her attempt of light humour

"I would now like to share it with you: "A bad habit never disappears miraculously; it's an undo-it-yourself project."

Everyone laughed again.

June could tell by looking at their faces that they found a profound meaning in the quote, such as she had. "I hope this quote is as much an inspiration to you as it has been to me."

As she sat down, Michael hugged her to him and kissed the top of her head. June had never felt more loved or accepted then she did by this group of people. She only hoped that this warm feeling could be passed on to others who would benefit from a little encouragement and support.

• • •

JUNE ARRIVED EARLY to work. She figured it would enable her to learn and work through the workload with plenty of time so that she didn't become too overwhelmed with it all. Amy, June's predecessor had some complications with her pregnancy. The condition was called Pre-Eclampsia, and it was causing her blood pressure to rise way too high. The obstetrician had also found traces of protein in her urine. This meant that her kidneys weren't working properly and it was placing enormous stress on herself and the baby.

The doctor had admitted her to hospital where she would stay until the birth. The baby's heart rate would constantly be measured on a fetal monitor, so that any sign of distress could be detected and acted upon immediately. If Amy's blood pressure could not be reduced, the baby would have to be induced earlier then the proposed due date or removed surgically.

To June the whole scenario of pregnancy was unfamiliar if not a little daunting, but she sympathized with Amy. There could be nothing more scary then carrying a child that you and your partner had created and had lived inside you for over eight months, to find right at the end there was a risk to its survival.

Before Amy had received the medical scare, it had been arranged that she spend three weeks with June, showing her the "ropes" of the job and familiarizing her with the company's procedures and routines. June had only spent a week and a half with Amy. In that time they had hit it off really well. Amy was a very good teacher. She was also very organized and thorough which June took on board. June was grateful that Amy had been such a good teacher in the short time they had worked together as she would have found herself in an even worse predicament then she was now.

Amy told June that she could ring her at the hospital if she had any queries at all. But June didn't want to disturb her. Charlotte Sinclair had also offered to assist June with any queries that she might have, but Charlotte was so incredibly busy that June found it was hard to catch her at any one given time.

June persevered and slowly but surely, everything began to unfold and make more sense. She had no trouble with the switchboard, she had previously used one and operating the computer was straightforward. June thought herself to be fairly technical minded so that area didn't phase her much. If she could just remember all the client contacts and different departments of the business, she would be alright. These were areas of the job that would only come with time and experience.

June's hard work was paid off when she received her first pay cheque. It was much more then she expected, so she was pleasantly surprised, and decided to call Michael and ask him out to dinner. It would be her shout. Gee, it felt good to be independent again!

CHAPTER 21

The man who removes a mountain begins
by carrying away small stones.
Chinese Proverb

MICHAEL AND JUNE had a wonderful night out together. They wined and dined in style at a five star ala-carte restaurant in the city called *Maxims*. The occasion was extra special because June had received in the mail that day, a letter from her solicitor. A date had been set for the divorce settlement. It was to go ahead in a month's time. This meant that the house would be sold and divided equally between Barry and her. She would have to find a place to live, but now that she was in regular employment. She didn't think that that would pose too much of a problem. May had relayed her banking experience to June, giving her advice on how to manage her money. She had also explained what to do in preparation before applying for a housing loan. June had decided that she would invest the money until she had a work history of at least twelve months. After this period, she would have a substantial deposit and was hoping to approach the bank for a loan to purchase a property of her own.

"Have you decided on what you are going to have for main course?" June asked Michael as they shared an entrée of oysters Kilpatrick.

"I'm kind of stuck on the seafood theme," Michael said as he sucked and slurped an oyster out of its shell.

"Me too," June admitted. "What do you say we be really extravagant and order the seafood platter with cray-fish?" Her pretty blue eyes met with his green ones and they shared an intimate smile.

"Are you sure you can afford it?" he asked her with concern. He didn't want her to blow all her pay on him.

"Yeah, I can afford it. Let's splurge."

And they did. Anyone in the restaurant who saw them would see a happy couple that was very comfortable with each other. And who totally enjoyed each other's company.

They shared a serve of the restaurants banana, pecan caramel pie, taking turns in feeding one another. They were totally unrepentant in selecting such a high calorie dessert. They had both reached goal weight now. The message that Angela had drummed into them, as a future weight management plan was "everything in moderation." Now that they had said goodbye to all their friends there, they were on their own now.

When they arrived home and were safely inside, they embraced immediately. June noticed that it was getting harder not to succumb to the need for physical fulfilment. She wondered how much longer they could continue like this before it happened and she still wasn't sure if she was ready to take that step. Physically she was, she recognised the signs in her body as it ached for that contact. But emotionally she hoped they could wait a bit longer.

She wondered if Michael was experiencing the same turmoil that she was. June had never known a man existed such as Michael who was so considerate, patient and respective of a woman's wishes in the way that he was. He didn't pressure, he didn't demand but then he was Michael. He was special.

"You know I love you, don't you?" He confessed to her as he nuzzled the hair on the back of her head.

She didn't know. But she was glad he had told her. It felt so good to be wanted.

"And I love you," she admitted, to him and herself for the first time. She turned around to face him and they kissed deeply, sealing their newly exposed feelings for one another.

CHAPTER 22

Mother's are the most instinctive philosophers.
Harriet Beecher Stowe

JUNE AND MICHAEL were having dinner at the William's house. As they sat around the table eating a succulent roast lamb and gravy they discussed the holiday to Europe that Ron and Shirl were embarking on in March, next year. They were going to be away for six weeks. Ron had applied for a retirement package. It had been accepted and he was due to finish work at the end of the year.

"Now we will be able to do all the things we have always wanted to do," Shirl told everyone.

"As long as you bring us back lots of presents," May said.

"And send lots of postcards," June added.

"We'll see what we can do," Ron said smiling.

When they had cleared all dishes from the table and stacked the dishwasher. They all adjourned to the family room, where they read through the tourism magazines together. Ron and Shirl explained the tours they would be taking, whilst they sipped percolated coffee.

June was feeling uneasy. May seemed to have cornered Michael and had been chatting to him most of the night. Her body language was showing all the signs of attraction and on occasion she was affectionately touching his arm and giggling at some of the things he was saying. Panic rushed through June. Michael's back was turned away from her so she couldn't read his expression, but images of the Mandy and Barry scenario flashed through her mind. She felt physically ill.

Unaware of the cause of her discomfort, April came over to chat with her oldest sister. "Are you feeling all right? You look a bit pale," she said.

"I think I'm coming down with something," June replied not wanting to jump to conclusions or overreact. But inside her stomach felt like it was on a rollercoaster, tunnelling deeper into a pit of fear to rise up again and plummet down once more.

"That's the last thing you need when you have just started a new job."

"I'll be okay. I just need an early night in bed. So anyway, how is the romance with the married teacher?" June asked her

April scrunched up her face before answering June's question. "Okay. I guess."

June decided to leave it at that. April obviously didn't want to elaborate any further. June suspected that there must be more to the story than April was letting on. She looked around the room for Michael. He wasn't there. Where was May? The panic rose till she almost burst with anxiety. Then Michael and Ron walked into the house from the back door.

"What have you guys been up to?" April asked them.

"I have been showing Michael my 'Baby,'" Ron said. He was referring to the Phase three, XY- GT Falcon in his garage. His father had left it to him in his will and it was his pride and joy.

"She's a beauty," Michael admitted.

"There's a disadvantage to living in a houseful of woman. But, Dad's finally found a kindred spirit," May said from the kitchen, she had been there all the time.

Both men laughed.

"Michael," June called out desperately. "I want to go home now. I don't feel too good . . ." She attempted to stand. Her head felt cloudy and she lost balance, falling back into the chair. Shirl, realising something wasn't right, came over and sat next to June.

"Are you okay?" Shirl asked as sat by her side and cradled June's head in her lap.

"I'll get you a glass of water," April offered as she made her way towards the kitchen.

"And I'll get a cool flannel to put behind your neck," May said. May was first to come back with the flannel. "Here you are June. Do you think you will be sick?" She placed the flannel in June's hand.

Michael watched June from across the room as the women fussed over her. Her complexion was deathly pale, and he was concerned for her. Shirl placed her hand on June's forehead.

"She doesn't appear to have a fever," she announced.

"I just want to go home," June protested. She was appreciative of the fuss everyone was making of her, but she just wanted to get home to her own bed and sleep.

"Come on then," Michael said as he picked her up and carried her to the car. He placed her in the seat and buckled her seatbelt. May passed June's handbag, which Michael placed on the floor beneath her. Shirl came out and placed a blanket over her to keep the warmth in. June was appreciative of this because her whole body had started to shiver. She felt frozen to the bone.

"You should take this just in case you need it," April said, placing a bowl onto June's lap.

"Now look after your self, June" Shirl said.

"Hope you're feeling better tomorrow," Ron said kissing her on the forehead.

When they arrived home, Michael carried June into her bed. She was fast asleep in his arms when he placed her down on the mattress, undressed her, put her pyjamas on and tucked her under the covers. He put his own pyjamas on, climbed into bed and snuggled down next to her.

• • •

JUNE WOKE EARLY the next day. She was still feeling awful. The fear would not go away. What if she lost him? What if she gained all her weight back and he didn't want her anymore? What if someone else took him away? How much longer would he wait?

The fear was engulfing her, eating her alive. She also felt guilty. Everyone had made a fuss of her last night and she was behaving like a child. She had to get a control of herself.

Michael was sitting at the kitchen table reading the paper. He thought he had heard her stir so he went into the bedroom to check on her. He lay down beside her and caressed the curls on the front of her head with his hand.

"How are you feeling today?" he asked her. She looked deathly pale and he was concerned.

"Not too good," June admitted afraid to make direct eye contact and give herself away.

"You have probably been overdoing it a bit lately," he said.

She nodded.

"Would you like a cup of tea or coffee?" he asked.

"No thanks" She replied shakily She still felt like she wanted to be sick again. She swallowed a couple of times to settle her stomach. "A tea would be nice, thanks."

"Okay," he said as he kissed her forehead before going into the kitchen to make the tea. Later on in the afternoon Shirl rang to see how she was going.

"I still feel queasy," June admitted.

"Have you eaten anything?" Shirl asked her. Food was always a priority to Shirl.

"I couldn't stomach anything at the moment. Michael asked me if I wanted breakfast this morning and it made me dry retch," June told her.

"Lucky it's the weekend," Shirl said.

"I know. The last thing I want is to have time off work. Charlotte is such a trooper. I don't think she has ever had a sick day in her life."

"Still, if you are not feeling better by Monday, you should probably see a doctor," Shirl recommended, adopting a maternal tone.

"Yeah you're probably right," June's voice started to drift off. She was feeling *so* confused.

"You know Michael loves you June?" Shirl said.

June was stunned into silence. Could her mother read her mind?

"He loves you. I know you were worried about May talking to him but that is because you have had a bad experience. To the rest of us, he only has eyes for you." A sob escaped and June felt the tears fall down her face. Was she that transparent?

"May said to me after you left that she wishes she could find a man that looks at her with love like Michael looks at you. He is so totally comfortable with his feelings for you, that he is not afraid who sees it."

June grabbed a tissue from the bedside table next to her and juggled the phone receiver in her other hand while attempting to dam the torrential downpour of emotion that was flowing from her eyes. "Do you think he knew . . . that I . . ." she stammered between sobs.

"No only I noticed. It's a mother's intuition. You'll understand one day."

"But I thought . . . I thought it was like Barry . . . and . . ."

"You need to realise that you have *changed* June. You'll always be June to me, my daughter. But you have gained so much confidence now. I should have been more conscious of the type of food I was feeding you girls. I blame myself for it in some ways. You're a great inspiration to me, to all of us. We are *so* proud of you - In fact I am going to join the *Calorie Counters* when I get back from Europe. I've already made the appointment . . ."

"Oh Mum, that is *so* great. I wish I could give you a big hug right now."

"Me *too* sweetheart, you know I'm always here for you?" She blew a kiss down the line and June reciprocated.

After she replaced the phone back on the cradle, June reflected on her mother's insight into her own feelings. She felt like a huge weight had been lifted off her shoulders.

CHAPTER 23

Where will I be in five years from now? I delight in not knowing. That's one of the greatest things about life- Its wonderful surprises.

Marlo Thomas

Throughout the week at work June felt strangely refreshed and at peace with herself. She carried on her day as if she had a new lease on life. Well, she supposed in a lot of ways she did. A lot of water had flowed under the bridge since her disastrous marriage with Barry. Even a clairvoyant couldn't have predicted the complete turnaround that had occurred in her life—full circle. The phone rang, distracting her thoughts. It was Michael.

"I know it's usually our night off from one another, but do you think you are up to going out to dinner tonight at Maxim's?" he asked her. The memory of the oysters and crayfish they had enjoyed when they had last dined there caused intense hunger pains in June's stomach. She could not think of a more perfect way to end this new and wonderfully perfect day.

"I'd love to," she answered, feeling unbelievingly happy and excited about seeing the man she loved so soon again. He made arrangements to collect her later on that evening and she sent him on his way with promises of love and good company.

As she dressed for the evening, she noticed a bundled up pile of material on the bottom of her wardrobe. She picked it up and discovered that it was one of the awful garments that she used to wear when she was very overweight. It barely resembled a dress and for curiosity sake, she stepped inside it trying it on. It was massive. She could fit her legs in the arm holes and still there was room for two more sets. She wrapped the stretched waistband around her and it covered her body twice. Elated she removed the dress and was about to throw it away when another thought occurred to her. She would keep it. A reminder of what was then and what was now, so she never became too complacent with herself again.

When Michael arrived to pick her up she rushed out to greet him.

"Hey. What's the hurry? Don't I even get a kiss hello?" he asked as he gently caught her in his arms and pulled her into an embrace; then swung her around so that he could get a proper look at her. "You look absolutely breathtaking."

"Thanks," she blushed. She was still not totally comfortable with compliments but she knew that Michael meant it. The hunger that burned in his eyes revealed a hunger that went way beyond lust. "Sorry for the rush," June apologized." It's just that I'm so looking forward to tonight."

"Me too." He grinned discreetly as he thought of the secret arrangements he had made for the evening.

At the restaurant Michael ordered a shrimp cocktail for entrée and the seafood basket for main course. June accepted his offer of wine, leaving the decision making up to him. She felt so relaxed and comfortable she was determined to sit back and go with the flow.

Suddenly, the lights in the restaurant dimmed and from out of nowhere a string quartet started to play softly in the background. The waiter placed the shrimp cocktails in front of them as well as a small dish with what looked like a red velvet cushion on top of it. He handed June a scroll that was neatly tied up with a gold ribbon.

Puzzled, June looked up at Michael. What is it . . . ?"

"Go on, open it," he encouraged her.

She did. On closer inspection, June noticed that it was some sort of invitation. "What's this for . . . ?

"Just read it," Michael coerced her, the green of his eyes intensely boring into her blue ones, not once blinking or breaking contact. "Read it aloud."

"Your company is requested . . . to attend the wedding of . . . she paused, looking up at him and he was momentarily struck by her beauty and how much she meant to him.

"Keep going," he demanded almost impatiently.

" . . . Michael Carrington and June McLeod . . . on the . . ." Her heart stopped then kicked in again at what seemed like one hundred beats per second. "Oh!" she exclaimed, choked up and lost for words. She turned to her left to find Michael beside her on his knees.

"June Mc Cleod, I was wondering if you will do me the honour of being my wife?"

June looked up into his face, which was beaming under the candlelight on the table. She had tears in her eyes as she listened intently to what he was saying. Michael reached across the table, and gently lifted the velvet cushion so that it was supported by both hands. Due to the dimmed light, June could not at this stage make out its exact contents.

"I understand that it is probably too soon. But I also know that in ten years I will still want to marry you as much as I do now if not more. And I am willing to wait until then if I have to. If that's what you want?"

As she looked into his eyes she knew that it was the right decision to make and that she loved this man almost more then life itself. She cleared her throat. Took his hand in hers and looked deeply into his sea green eyes. "I will have to check my diary, but I'm pretty sure that day is free" she teased.

"Is that a yes?" he asked as he placed an emerald cut diamond ring on her finger. He looked tortured and June decided it was time to put him out of his misery.

"It most defiantly is, Michael Carrington" she assured him. "I believe I am ready."

THE END

You can do anything you set your mind to, man

Eminem- from the song 'Lose yourself,' Shady Records

Tate Publishing & *Enterprises*

Tate Publishing is commited to excellence in the publishing industry. Our staff of hightly trained professionals, including editors, graphic designers, and marketing personnel, work together to produce the very finest books available. The company reflects the philosophy established by the founders, based on Psalms 68:11,

"THE LORD GAVE THE WORD AND GREAT WAS THE COMPANY OF THOSE WHO PUBLISHED IT."

If you would like further information, please call
1.888.361.9473
or visit our website
www.tatepublishing.com

Tate Publishing & *Enterprises*, LLC
127 E. Trade Center Terrace
Mustang, Oklahoma 73064 USA